# SASHA PALEY

# HUGE

## WITHDRAWN
## FROM STOCK

**SIMON AND SCHUSTER**

First published in Great Britain in 2008 by Simon & Schuster UK Ltd
Africa House, 64–78 Kingsway, London WC2B 6AH
A CBS COMPANY

www.simonsays.co.uk

Originally published in 2007 by Simon & Schuster Books for Young Readers,
An imprint of Simon & Schuster Children's Publishing Division, New York

A CIP catalogue record for this book
is available from the British Library.

ISBN: 978-1-84738-137-8

1 3 5 7 9 10 8 6 4 2

Printed and bound in Great Britain by
Cox & Wyman Ltd, Reading, Berkshire.

# CHAPTER 1

**DATE:** June 28th

**FOOD:** 1 Snickers bar and 3 red gummi
bears while H. wasn't looking

**EXERCISE:** Bite me.

"FASTER, FASTER!" WIL HOPKINS'S TRAINER, HEATHER, YELLED OVER
the sound of crashing waves.

Wil groaned, her feet sinking deeper into the soft Malibu
sand. She could just barely see the freshly painted white steps
that led up to her cliff-side oceanview house. They sparkled in
the distance.

"C'mon, you can do it!" Heather punched her fists in the
air like a prizefighter. Heather had been leading Wil on mile-
long power walks for exactly one year, eight months, three days,
and forty-eight minutes. And for exactly that long, Heather had
to push, prod, and beg Wil to finish that last quarter mile.

"We're almost there!" Heather enthused as Wil's house
came into full view, the only house in Malibu with an enormous jewel-encrusted sword pitched among its palm trees.
It looked like a giant had been killed there hundreds of years

1

ago and the sword was a last reminder of an ancient war. In reality, the sword was circa 2004 and a symbol for the family business, Excalibur Sport and Health Club. Heather was Wil's parents' star trainer. She never broke a sweat on their power walks, and Wil often fantasized about murdering her with that oversized sword by the time they got to this spot on the beach.

Wil had successfully ditched her previous trainer, Ty, but there was no shaking Heather. At first, Ty's slender physique and *very* cute southern accent had inspired Wil to keep up—and she'd secretly hoped that Malibu's perfectly tanned and toned girls sprawled out on their expensive blankets might mistake him for her boyfriend, at least from a distance. But when he told her that in order to really lose the weight, she would have to cut out sugar *altogether,* Wil complained to her parents that Ty looked at her in a way that made her . . . *uncomfortable.* But all her parents did was switch out Ty for Heather, and Wil knew there was a whole long list of Excalibur's trainers ready to step in and replace her at any time.

Heather put her sneakered foot on the bottom step of the white-painted stairs that led up, up, up to Wil's house and motioned for Wil to go ahead.

"You first." Wil tried to catch her breath and stared at the white stairs looming above her.

Heather shook her head, her perky brunette ponytail swaying from side to side. "I'm going for a run."

"No Pilates today?" Wil asked, trying not to sound winded.

Heather almost always ended the power walk with a session in the sweaty, stinky sunroom her parents called the Pilates Palace.

"Small flood in the palace, I guess," Heather explained. "So I guess I'll see you when you get back." Not looking Wil in the eye, Heather propped up one of her feet on the railing and stretched her hamstrings. Two guys jogging by on the beach slowed to stare at her. "And don't worry, you're gonna do great!"

The hot sun glared down on Wil. She took a long swig of water from her almost-empty Nalgene bottle and gazed longingly up at her air-conditioned house. "Do great at what?" she asked distractedly.

"Wellness Canyon." Heather straightened up and held the rail for balance as she flexed her perfectly toned calves. "I probably won't even recognize you when I see you again," she said.

"I'm not going to Wellness Canyon." Wil laughed, thinking of the glorified fat camp her parents had been talking about all year. She looked toward her palatial Spanish-style house with the top-floor wing where she knew her brand new PowerBook and flat-screen TV were waiting for her. No *way* was she missing a summer of that.

A look of confusion spread across Heather's face before finally becoming one of comprehension. "Right. Well, uh, anyway, have fun," she said as she began jogging backward.

Heather was a pink splotch way down on the beach before Wil got halfway up the steps, her thick legs throbbing. She'd thrown away every one of the Wellness Canyon brochures her parents had placed around the house. She despised the pictures of fake girls all pretending life was great and that no one was fat. Just this morning she'd burned one in the sink in her parents' bathroom, leaving the ashes for them to find.

Wil wheezed as the top step came into focus. She stopped and grabbed the rail, catching her breath. Then she hoisted herself up the final few stairs, her face red from anger as much as from the exertion.

She pushed the sliding glass doors open, expecting to find her parents sucking down their twice-daily cocktails of Excalibur-brand vitamins and supplements, but the front room was empty. As she made her way down the all-glass hall toward the Pilates Palace, a whirring sound filled her ears. Outside, a gray van with the words MALIBU PLUMBING AND SPRINKLER idled, its yellow hose snaking its way toward the house.

Just then her mother emerged from the Pilates Palace at the end of the hall. She was wearing an aqua spandex leotard and a Max Mara hoodie and holding a clump of dripping carpet. "Hi, honey, how was your workout?"

"What happened?" Wil asked, momentarily distracted from her outrage.

"Our bathroom sink caused a leak in the wall of the palace," her mother explained.

Her father appeared, grossly shirtless, holding an even bigger chunk of wet carpet. "Did Heather leave for her run already?" he asked, the carpet dripping on his aqua biking shorts. Wil noticed for the first time that her parents were wearing *matching* spandex. Ew. "I wanted to join her."

"Why did you guys tell her that I was going to Wellness Canyon?" Wil demanded, remembering why she'd come here.

Her parents exchanged a look.

"I already told you I wasn't going." Wil's voice rose as the afternoon sun filtered down through the skylight. "I'm not going to spend the summer at some camp doing sit-ups and watching a bunch of fat kids measure out serving sizes of cereal. Besides, I already have tickets for the Decemberists concert, so I can't go."

"Honey, it's for the best, really," her father said calmly, standing on his tiptoes and flexing his calves.

It might have been a funny scene—her parents in their impeccable workout gear, holding pieces of soggy carpet—if they hadn't been talking about something as horrid as shipping their daughter off to some kind of militant boot camp for the entire summer.

"I'm not going to fat camp." She crossed her thick arms over her ample chest. The ocean sparkled through the Pilates Palace's floor-to-ceiling windows. A brilliant-white sandpiper glided by, and out on the water she could see a couple of colorful sailboats, floating in the breeze. Wil scowled. She couldn't believe her parents thought she'd leave all of this behind for some idiotic camp filled with a bunch of fatties.

"You *are* going, and that's the end of it." Her mother smiled and maneuvered past Wil to deposit the carpet in the hallway. "But it's not fat camp, sweetie—it's a weight-loss *spa*."

Wil leaned against the clean white wall, hoping that her back would leave a big, sweaty mark. "Since when do you tell me what to do?"

"You don't have a choice on this one, kiddo." Her father sniffed at the wet carpet and then wrinkled his nose before moving past Wil and dropping it in the hallway. "It's for your own good."

"No, it's not." Wil turned around to face her parents and pressed her shoulders against the wall. She felt the sweat start to cool the inside of her thighs as the air-conditioning reached them.

Her father placed a hand on her mother's shoulder. They presented a disgusting show of solidarity in their matching turquoise workout gear.

"Fine." Wil turned and stomped down the hall, nearly running into the plumber, who flattened against the wall to let her by. She could not freaking *believe* her parents were sending her to fat camp. They could call it whatever they wanted, but she'd be damned if she was going to count rice cakes or drink seaweed protein shakes or share her feelings about being overweight or give her parents the satisfaction—and then a lightbulb went off over her sweaty brunette head. A bright, glittering, beautiful lightbulb.

"That's just fine," she said, turning around to face her parents. "But mark my words: I'll be the only girl in the history of Wellness Canyon to *gain* weight!" And then she turned back around, a determined grin spreading across her face.

6

# CHAPTER 2

**DATE:** June 29th

**FOOD:** 1 piece of celery, 1 tbsp. peanut butter, and 3 raisins

**EXERCISE:** Five sit-ups before bed. Three push-ups (knees on ground)

APRIL ADAMS WOKE UP AT THE CRACK OF DAWN, EXCITEMENT quivering through every part of her. She'd already packed and repacked her bag eight times—going through her closet last week, she'd come across the vintage striped duffel bag her father had given her before he went to work one day when she was five and never returned. Her mother never talked about him, but she kept his picture in a silver frame on the dresser in the bedroom. April would sometimes sneak in there and stare at it, feeling her face for her father's chiseled jaw and cheekbones. *They're in there somewhere,* she'd think.

April wanted to be sure the things she'd packed were going to be trendy yet practical, cool without trying too hard. Since school had ended, she'd torn her closet apart, looking for clothes that were Wellness Canyon–worthy. She'd studied the packing list scrupulously, and her bag was perfectly stocked with a little bit of everything—several pairs of black Adidas shorts like the ones super-popular Olivia St. James wore in gym class, a brand-new pack of pink XXL Jockey for Her tees, plenty of khaki shorts, four button-downs—all in several sizes to accommodate her weight loss for the summer.

April had also packed something else: a pair of Habitual jeans in a *way* small size that she'd miraculously found on the sale rack at Nordstrom. They were expensive, gorgeous, and still wrapped neatly in the fancy department store tissue paper. And they were decidedly *not* fat-girl jeans.

The smell of grease wafted up to her room and April paused, waiting to hear the motorized hum of her mother's Rascal from the cramped kitchen below. April sighed. She loved her mom, but in her most bitter moments—usually standing on a scale and peering down at the numbers hovering around two hundred— April blamed her mom for her own weight problem.

Before her mother went on disability last year, dinner had consisted of whatever was five for five dollars at one of the fast-food restaurants between their house and Sprague Plastics, where her mom had worked. April had unwrapped three meals a day for as long as she could remember, and each year, she'd gotten bigger and unhappier. And so had her mom.

"Breakfast is ready, honey!" her mother's voice called from the kitchen.

April heaved the duffel bag over her shoulder and took a

final look in the full-length mirror at the foot of her bed. Her stomach bulged over the edges of her dark green khaki shorts, and her puffy upper arms sagged out the sides of her pink-striped polo shirt. But April smiled. *Not for long,* she thought.

As soon as April stepped into the kitchen, Cleo, their also overweight black cat, waddled over to her, purring and rubbing her face happily against April's ankles. She meowed up at April, who leaned down to scratch Cleo's chin. "You could lose some weight too, fat girl," April muttered in her kitty voice.

"Mom, there isn't time for breakfast," April complained, refusing to take a seat at the yellow Formica table. The plastic seats stuck to the back of her legs, so April often ate standing up.

"The bus doesn't leave for another hour." Her mother was dressed in her typical shapeless navy blue cotton sweat suit, her recently permed hair lying in short, tight curls around her face. She had a smear of dried pancake batter on her large round glasses. April's mom reversed her Rascal and opened the refrigerator door, peering inside at the crammed shelves. April dropped her bag and reluctantly sank down into a chair.

"This is your last chance to load up on the good stuff!" Her mom leaned over the side of her Rascal to grab the bottle of Aunt Jemima syrup from one of the shelves.

April examined the crowded breakfast table—three huge stacks of pancakes dripping with melting butter, white toast, several different kinds of jams and jellies, a giant bowl of scrambled eggs smothered in Velveeta cheese, and a plate of greasy bacon that wasn't even soaking on a paper towel.

9

April swallowed nervously. "I'm not hungry," she said, still staring at the strips of bacon—blackened, just as she liked them. She sat on her hands to keep from taking one.

Her mother looked up from their old olive green refrigerator, a hurt look spreading across her face. "But you have to eat breakfast. It's a long trip."

"It's only a couple hours away." April forced a note of kindness into her voice.

"But you have to eat," her mother insisted. "If you don't want it now, I can wrap it up and—"

"No!" April yelled. Her mother looked startled and April immediately softened a little. "Mom, I saved all year for this— *all* of my birthday money. Christmas. Everything."

Her mother's wide brown eyes focused on April's face as she scooted her Rascal away from the fridge toward the little food-covered table.

"And that means I just . . . I really want this to work." April rubbed the red-and-white-plaid tablecloth in between her thumb and forefinger to keep her hands busy. She didn't want to be tempted by anything on the table.

"Oh, honey, I like you just the way you are." The syrup bottle slipped out of her mother's hand and skittered across the linoleum. She paused and bent down to retrieve it, her short, stubby fingers reaching for the upside-down bottle.

April got up quickly and grabbed the syrup bottle, not wanting to see her mother struggle. She sat back down.

Her mother snatched a piece of bacon from the table, blew

on it, and put it in her mouth. April watched her chew and lick her lips. "Have a piece of toast, at least?" her mother asked pleadingly.

April grabbed two slices of unbuttered toast, smiled tightly, and pushed away from the table. Her mother began to put everything into Tupperware and shove it to the back of the fridge. "Let's just go, okay?"

April pushed open the door to the garage. Her mother's walker was folded up in the corner and an old wheelchair, from before her mom got the Rascal, hung lopsided on the wall. In the corner stood the rickety wooden shelves that held their bulk food purchases from Costco: macaroni and cheese, twelve-packs of soda, tubs of mayo and peanut butter. It was like April's whole life was just sitting there staring back at her. And she couldn't wait to start over.

Her mother rode down the ramp that led from their utility room to the garage. "Honey, when you've loaded your things, can you help me with the Rascal?"

April dropped her bag on the passenger's seat and sighed as she went to help her mother into their van. April waited, holding the Rascal steady while her mother scooted into the driver's seat.

"Ready?" her mother asked, breathing heavily as she started up the van. They backed out of the driveway and April said a silent goodbye to the small, squat house.

The ride to the Greyhound station was mercifully short, and April stuck her arm out the window, feeling the rush of the wind between red lights. Her mother switched on the local pop station and began singing along to a cheesy Clay Aiken song. April smiled and joined in, harmonizing to the familiar tune. Her mom turned up the volume and reached over to pat April on the leg.

Finally, the bus station came into view up ahead and April grabbed the strap of her duffel bag. "Take care of Cleo, okay?" She hated to think of the two of them alone together, eating to make themselves feel less lonely.

"Hold on," her mother said as a McDonald's commercial came on the radio. "I'll get out with you."

"That's okay," April said quickly. She placed a sweaty hand on the door handle. "You don't have to. I can just jump out."

Her mother pulled into a parking spot and let the van idle. "I can put your bag on my cart and carry it for you," she offered. "It looks heavy." She reached over and fumbled to unbuckle the seat belt from underneath the overhang of her stomach.

"No, really. It's fine." April looked over at the groups of people milling about the station. She turned back to her mom, forcing her voice to be bright. "Mom, maybe you won't even recognize me when I get back!"

April's mother smiled, the smear of pancake batter still visible on her glasses. "Oh, honey." She tapped her chubby fingers against the steering wheel. "Just try to have fun."

"It's not for fun." April heard the disappointment in her voice as she tugged the oversized duffel up off the floor.

"Well, try to have fun anyway," her mother said absentmindedly. "And don't forget to call or write as much as you can." She blinked quickly. "I'm going to miss you so much."

April leaned over, kissed her cheek, and hopped out of the van, slamming the door behind her. Her mother waved desperately and April blew her one last kiss before turning her back. Up ahead, the hulking gray bus that would carry her away from a summer of sausages and pancakes and late-night snacks and bags of potato chips idled in its bay. In six weeks she'd return to San Luis Obispo wearing her skinny jeans. Her mom would probably recognize her . . . but maybe no one else would. At least, that's what she hoped.

She handed her bag and ticket to the driver and got on the bus, finding a window seat toward the back. April allowed herself one quick look at her mom's van—and her old life—before facing forward, a small smile breaking out across her face.

# CHAPTER 3

**DATE:** June 29th

**FOOD:** 2 packs of Reese's peanut butter cups

**EXERCISE:** Does hiding from my parents so I wouldn't have to come here count?

"WELCOME TO WELLNESS CANYON." WIL READ THE LARGE SIGN on the huge iron gate from the backseat of a town car. Her chauffeur maneuvered up a long, tree-lined drive toward a cheesy replica of a mountain lodge. A line of BMWs, Mercedes SUVs, and Volvos idled under an American flag flapping in the wind high above the long pebbled driveway. At the end of it was a parking area, and to Wil's left, she could see a large green lawn, already swarming with overweight teenagers. A clear blue lake sparkled in the distance beyond the lawn, and a series of bluffs carved out of red rocks surrounded the entire camp.

After refusing to pack this morning, Wil was over an hour late for check-in, but she didn't care. She crawled out of the car and looked around. An overly eager counselor spotted Wil and ran over, clipboard in hand. *Welcome! Your name?* Wil read her lips, the sound of the Shins filling her ears at full volume. Wil made the counselor repeat her question before finally pulling out her earbuds and telling the woman her name.

"You're in Franklin House, room four," the counselor said enthusiastically, as if Wil had won some sort of fabulous prize. "We're at the Lodge now." She pointed at the building behind her. "You'll go past the spa building and take a left when the path forks."

Wil trudged off without thanking her. She pulled her Louis Vuitton suitcase up the long pebbled path, the logos covered with stickers of her favorite bands. Inside were about fifteen candy bars hidden in socks and the pockets of her shorts and also eight jumbo-sized shampoo bottles loaded with M&M's, Reese's Pieces, Skittles, and other candy Wil had decided was shower-friendly. The wheels kept catching on the rocks and grass as she wandered past the open lawn and down another long tree-lined path.

It turned out Franklin House was blissfully far from the Lodge, the lawn and, Wil hoped, everyone and everything. Wil planned to miss all meals and activities and barricade herself in her room for the duration of the summer. With any luck, no one would even know she was there. Wil pulled her bag up the steps onto the long porch of Franklin. She walked along the shady wooden porch until she stopped in front of room 4.

She paused and said a little prayer that her roommate was already out on one of the "exhilarating adventures" the brochure had promised. Instead, Wil opened the door to find a large girl in a pink button-down standing on one of the single beds. The girl had very shiny auburn hair that was held back with a pink ribbon and a smattering of freckles across her nose. Despite her weight, the girl was actually quite pretty. She held a string of twinkling Christmas lights against the wall with one hand and a roll of tape in the other.

"You're here!" her new roommate squeaked. "I was beginning to wonder if something happened to you!"

The girl plopped down off the bed, leaving the string of lights hanging off the wall. "I'm April. Your roommate—but I guess you already knew that!"

Wil blinked and looked around the room. The space was definitely smaller than Wil's bedroom at home and held not one but *two* small twin beds, a mere ten feet apart. At the far end of the room, there were a desk, a large paned window, and, okay, a beautiful view, but nonetheless, the room was practically uninhabitable.

"You're Wilhelmina, right?" April asked, clearly knowing the answer.

Wil cringed at the sound of her full name. "Just Wil."

"Nice to meet you." April stuck out her hand. Wil stared at it and then shook it tentatively. She couldn't tell if April's hand was sweaty or if it was her own.

"I thought I'd take this side of the room." April motioned toward a bed that looked like it had already been slept in. A nest of personal items was strewn across the blankets and a nightstand. "Of course, unless you want it."

Wil shrugged. "Whatever." She hoisted her bag up onto the empty bed, the taupe blanket tucked neatly under a fluffed pillow. A clump of grass dislodged from the wheels and landed on the shiny floor. On the pillow was a small pink spiral-bound notebook with the Wellness Canyon palm tree logo on the front. Wil picked it up and flipped through the pages. Each page had blanks ready to be filled in for the date, food and exercise, and the completely ridiculous "How I'm feeling."

"Mine's purple. And we have matching pens too!" April ran over to the shared desk and thrust out a pink ballpoint for Wil. "And here's the Wellness Canyon Attaché," she read off an enormous folder, completely mangling the word. "I've practically memorized all the rules and stuff already. Meals are eight, noon and six, no snacking in between. Laundry pickup is weekly, if you've elected for that service. We have free time every night, although sometimes there are like, movies and stuff. They post the info in the dining hall. What else? There are only three weigh-ins all summer, so that we don't get that hung up on that kind of thing. They said that they want it to be a 'lifestyle change,' although *puh-lease*, I can't wait to see the pounds melting off." April grabbed at a roll of stomach bulge. "Oh, and the honor system is, like, super-important here." She finally finished.

Wil ignored April and lay back on her bed, not bothering to unpack. She liked the idea of keeping all her clothes and things in her suitcase just in case the opportunity to flee came up. She closed her eyes as April climbed back up on her bed to finish affixing the Christmas lights to the walls.

"Did you know they don't even measure your food? They just, like, trust you to make good decisions," April told her, straining to tape the lights to the ceiling. "I guess everyone just wants to be here so badly they stick to it." April didn't seem to notice that Wil hadn't responded to a single thing she had said. "So where are you from?"

Wil wondered if she could feign sleep and considered letting out a snore. Instead, she turned on her side and stared out the window at the red rocks in the distance. "Actually, I already know you're from Malibu," April said, giggling. "I asked the counselor about you and she told me. What's it like there? Oh, you don't mind some candles, do you?" Wil craned her neck and watched April sprinkle the room with tiny votive candles, dotting the windowsill and the bookshelf. She wondered how long this girl could keep up the stream of her one-sided conversation.

"Have you ever seen Brad Pitt? I once saw a picture of Cameron Diaz running on the beach in Malibu in *Us Weekly*. It didn't really look like her, though. I bet they touch up those pictures. That's what my mother says, anyway. I believe it, too. Did you ever notice that all the women in magazines practically have the same body? Of course, not that I would mind. But that's why we're here, isn't it?" April took a slight pause, and Wil's hopes rose that April was finally done with her tirade.

"Do you surf? I heard it's great exercise. You know, gets your heart rate up."

No luck.

Wil reached into the hand-crocheted purse she'd bought at a flea market in West Hollywood and pulled out her Bose earbuds. She slipped them in as April droned on about how much she'd like to visit Malibu, the discordant strains of the Decemberists drowning out her annoying roommate. Wil drifted off, hovering somewhere between relaxation and deep sleep before a mild tremor shook her awake. She bolted up, startled to find the same eager-beaver counselor from before standing over her, still holding a clipboard. Wil removed an earbud. "What?" she asked the counselor.

"I said, slip into something comfortable." The counselor smiled and clapped. "General fitness tests out on the lawn. Five minutes." She headed back out the door. "Oh, and be sure to bring your new notebooks!"

April smiled at Wil, practically bouncing as she checked herself out in the mirror. Then she launched back into her incessant monologue. "I can't believe we're finally here. Do you think that we'll be hiking today? Or maybe not yet. I read that they do some kind of icebreaker activities. That should b—"

Wil put her headphones back on, and it seemed April finally got the hint because she stopped talking. Unfortunately, she was now glowering at Wil instead. "What?" Wil asked loudly over the music blasting in her ears.

"Nothing. I just thought you'd want to go to orientation together or something." April looked a little hurt.

"Right," Wil said, rolling her eyes. "Look, I don't want to be friends. I don't even want to *be* here. As far as I'm concerned, this whole thing sucks. So just . . . go find someone who cares."

Wil turned her back to April and turned her iPod up as far as it could go. But it still wasn't loud enough to drown out the sound of April slamming the door behind her.

# CHAPTER 4

**DATE:** June 29th

**FOOD:** 3 apple slices and 1 rice cake. And does my vitamin count?

**EXERCISE:** Well, my bag _was_ really heavy....

APRIL FUMED AS SHE POWER-WALKED OUT OF FRANKLIN HOUSE and toward the lawn, the bright noon sun beating down on her. She'd been so eager to get away from her idiotic roommate, she'd forgotten to put on any of her new Neutrogena SPF 50 sunscreen, but there was no way she was going back to Franklin with Wil inside.

She ducked under a large tree for some shade and did a few quick hamstring stretches in preparation for the fitness tests. All of the other campers were spread out, milling around and stretching on the bright green freshly cut lawn. April looked out over the lawn at Lake Jennings, which sparkled like a sapphire in the distance. She nervously thought of her swimsuit—black and shapeless and huge—but then remembered where she was. There weren't going to be any Olivia St. Jameses stalking around with their size-two red bikinis hanging off their slim hips. She smiled again as she gazed at a glass-walled building close to the lake. She guessed it was the open-air spinning, Pilates, and yoga studio. Because she had been reading the brochures every day for nearly a year, she knew the fitness complex was over there somewhere—even if she couldn't see it from the lawn. April took a deep breath and then suddenly frowned when she caught sight of Wil straggling toward the hundred or so campers. She was still wearing her jeans.

"Jessica!" yelled a girl about fifteen pounds heavier than April. She practically galloped toward a circle of barely chubby girls gathered next to a large oak tree on the right side of the lawn. A girl with long blond hair blowing in the breeze turned around when she heard her name and gave a pretty smile to the heavy girl. The blond girl, Jessica, *barely* looked like she needed to lose weight at all. She was a little plump, sure, but she was practically April's *goal* weight.

"It's so good to see you!" The heavy girl puffed over to Jessica, beads of sweat dripping down her forehead.

Jessica tucked her shiny, perfectly straight hair behind her ears and reached to slap a bug on her leg. "You too, Megan."

April moved back into the sunlight and tucked her hair behind her ears too, smoothing it several times as she watched the girls hug hello. "Oh my God," Jessica said, suddenly looking toward April. The other girls all looked too, and April flushed with embarrassment.

"Colin!" Jessica called out, still looking over in April's direction. April almost waved, confused, but then a large boy—

more muscle-y than chubby—sprinted across one of the white pebbled pathways leading to the lawn and over to the group of girls by the tree. He was tall and big-boned, with light brown hair and striking blue eyes fringed by long dark lashes. He was wearing a fitted black-and-red T-shirt with the USC Trojans logo on the front and holding a bright green Frisbee in one hand.

"Hey, Jessie," Colin answered, holding out his arms. "How's it going, gorgeous?" Immediately, Jessica stepped away from the crowd of girls and ran to Colin.

Jessica kissed Colin on the cheek, a trail of chubby girls following behind her like little ducklings.

April willed herself not to stare at Jessica and Colin and instead looked around. The other campers were all loosely assembled around a bunch of blue-shirted counselors and a petite redhead in her early thirties. But then April saw a flash of blond hair out of the corner of her eye and turned to see Colin laughing with Jessica. Her light pink Adidas Originals looked adorable with her fitted V-neck and cropped yoga pants. On her ears, a pair of small diamonds sparkled in the sunlight. April reached up to her bare ears and removed her hair from behind them, covering up the fact that she wasn't wearing any earrings—let alone diamonds. Colin spun the Frisbee on his finger and said something that caused all the other girls in his immediate vicinity to burst into laughter.

One of the Barely Chubbies handed Jessica a tube of expensive-looking sunscreen. Jessica took it and neatly applied a stripe to each arm and one to her nose before smearing the lotion in with her hands. April knew this could be her chance to introduce herself and quite possibly make her first Wellness Canyon friends.

April took an eager step forward but then froze as a loud voice interjected from behind her, "This is pathetic."

April turned and saw Wil standing there with her hands on her hips. April didn't respond to her roommate, though. She definitely wasn't interested in agreeing with *anything* Wil said. April didn't have time for Wil's totally obvious negativity—not this summer, not when she was here to change her life.

"Gather round, everyone," the petite redhead called out from underneath the large oak tree. Despite her small size, her voice boomed over the large crowd. It was cheerful and perky and it made April want to do some extra jumping jacks right then just to prove that she belonged there. "Everyone make a big circle around me and the other counselors."

A lopsided oval of overweight campers slowly shuffled around her and the handful of blue-shirted, khaki-shorted counselors on either side of her. The leaves overhead rustled from the cool breeze coming off the lake.

"For those of you who didn't meet me at sign-in, I'm Melanie," the redhead said. A silver whistle hung around her neck on a thin black cord. "I'm the director here at Wellness Canyon." The counselors clapped automatically and a smattering of cheers went up in the circle from the girls—many of them the Barely Chubbies—who obviously had been to

Wellness Canyon before. April wasn't sure what to think about that. First of all, it made her a little sad that a lot of the cool kids already knew each other, which would just make it harder for someone new to hang out with them. She'd sort of thought they'd all be starting out on the same ground. But also, wasn't it kind of weird that some kids would come back here for another year? Did that mean they didn't lose all their weight last summer? April hoped their return was just a sign that they loved it so much here and that maybe they'd just been extra fat to begin with, although she couldn't really imagine Jessica as ever being huge.

Melanie reached into a large box next to her on the grass and pulled out a pair of humongous jeans that she held up. "These used to be mine. Size twenty-four. But thanks to Wellness Canyon—never again!" Everyone cheered and April was immediately mesmerized.

"Some of you have heard this before, but it bears repeating." Melanie's face became more serious and she put her hands on her hips. "You might look around and think that this is some sort of luxury resort." Melanie looked at their surroundings, nodding in approval, as if seeing them for the first time. Then she focused back on the crowd, her face again serious. "But looks can be deceiving. You all know that. We're here to work, right?"

The campers erupted in applause, April included. She glanced over at Wil, who was examining her fingernails as if there was something supremely interesting about her slightly chipped black polish. April wanted to jab her in the side to make her pay attention, but she didn't.

"That's right." Melanie smiled, looking proud of their enthusiasm. "We're here"—Melanie motioned to herself and the other counselors—"to push you to the limit. We're here to help you train your bodies *as well as* your minds." Melanie poked her forehead with a slim finger. "We all need to heal," she said, laying her hand across her heart. "Being overweight takes a toll not just on your body, but on every part of you."

Wil snorted loudly. April saw a few girls in front of them shoot glances over their shoulders. "If I puke, I promise I won't puke on your shoes," she told April loudly, leaning forward.

"Shhhhhh!" April hissed at Wil, glaring. Wil rolled her eyes but shut up. Above their heads, a small bird started twittering in the tree, as if scolding Wil.

"You're all going to face frustration here. What's ahead of you is not going to be easy." Melanie gripped her hands together like she was saying a prayer. "I can tell you right now that you're going to have plenty of amazing days. And I can promise you, those will outnumber the tough days." She tilted her head sympathetically, almost like the little bird still watching on the branch overhead. "But we're here to help you work through the frustrations. And if we're hard on you, it's because we want you to succeed. We want you to reach your full potential. We're on your side."

"Gag me with a Luna bar." Wil stuck one of her black fingernails in her mouth and pretended to gag. The two girls in front of them turned again, irritated looks on their faces. April took one step away from Wil and instead listened to Melanie, who was running through the daily schedule. A light breeze tickled April's skin, making the little blond hairs on her arms stand up straight.

"Kevin, can you hand me my water?" Melanie asked one of the counselors, who quickly proffered a pink Nalgene bottle that had a bumper sticker neatly placed on the side that said, SUGAR: THE GATEWAY DRUG. Melanie took a long gulp while the crowd shifted on the neat lawn. "Okay," she finally said, her voice recharged. "Here's how camp is going to work. You will have two scheduled group activities every day: one in the morning and one in the afternoon. These are mandatory. In addition, each of you will be spending two hours of every day in the gym. The time is up to you. You will be working with private trainers who will tailor an exercise program specifically for you. One that you can take back to your lives when this is over." Melanie clapped at her own statement and the other counselors quickly joined her.

"In addition, everyone will participate in three small competitions. These will lead up to the Wellness Canyon Olympics, which will be held at the end of summer. We'll be putting the teams together after we get the fitness test results. We want each team to be a mix of strengths and weaknesses. You'll find out who your teammates are in a couple of days."

"I call Colin!" someone yelled, and everyone, including Melanie, laughed. April looked at Colin, the guy in the USC

T-shirt, and saw him smile. April couldn't help but hope that she'd be on Colin's team too. He was heavy, but in a linebacker kind of way. April hadn't exactly ever done anything athletic besides stand off to the side of the basketball court, or volleyball court, or soccer field in gym class—the teacher was never mean enough to actually make her participate.

"All right." Melanie smiled as she quieted the group. "Most importantly, you need to learn to rely on your roommate. We've paired all of you up based on your personality profiles and summer goals. You are here to balance each other. For the rest of the summer, your roommate is your buddy for everything. You'll learn to act as a team, to support each other, and to succeed together. We'll do some trust activities to build those relationships, but most of the burden is on you. If you don't have a good relationship with your roommate, you *will fail.*" She smiled cheerfully, as if this was the best news she'd announced all day.

A cold chill ran down April's back as she looked over at Wil, who looked up from her fingernails. "Ha ha. Sucks to be you," Wil deadpanned, looking straight at her.

"*Be quiet,*" April muttered through gritted teeth. All around her, roommates were standing in pairs, looking like they were excitedly exchanging life stories and becoming friends. She wished with all her might that her roommate was anyone but Wil. Even the two largest guys in camp—together they probably weighed several hundred pounds—were standing together and laughing.

"Lastly," Melanie continued. "You probably wondered why

we had you bring these." She held up a small booklet, spiral bound at the top. "These are your food and exercise journals. You need to be accountable for how you treat your body and for how it feels. Record all of your exercises and everything you eat in here. Everything counts, no matter how small: you bite it, you write it. I repeat: you bite it, you write it!" Kevin ran around distributing light blue lanyards with the Wellness Canyon logo to each camper. April watched eagerly as Jessica clipped her little blue notebook to the lanyard, and she did the same.

"Okay, everybody," Melanie called, "pair up with your roommate in front of the Lodge and we'll get started." She raised a fist in the air and bounded through the crowd, leading them across the lawn toward the largest building at camp. It resembled a huge wooden mountain lodge—all wood and glass in clean, modern lines.

The crowd shuffled messily toward Melanie and Kevin as they passed the long ropes course and driveway. To the right of the Lodge, April could see the spa building. She could just picture her skinny self sitting in the sauna with Jessica and the other Barely Chubbies, all of them wrapped in cute towels and talking about boys.

"So, when do you think we start chopping wood, lumberjack?" A snarky voice snapped April back to attention. Wil's dark curly hair hung limply around her face.

"Look," April blurted, surprising herself with the stern tone in her voice. "Would it kill you to just be positive? I mean, why are you even here?"

"My parents sent me." Wil kicked at a pebble in the grass, sending it skidding into the sneaker of a camper in front of them. She turned her striking blue eyes on April. If April didn't hate the implications of it, she would have told Wil she had very pretty eyes. But when you're fat and someone tells you your eyes are pretty, it just means they think the rest of you is *not* so pretty. April was always getting complimented on her eyes. "Why are *you* here?"

"Because I want to be." April shrugged and looked over at Jessica and Colin's group. Jessica was arm in arm with another girl, laughing, and April felt a lump rise in her throat. *That's* how her summer was supposed to be. Not spent with someone like Wil.

"Well, I'm happy the way I am," Wil said easily.

April stopped and turned around, looking Wil in the eye. April pressed her hands into the rolls of fat pouring out over the top of her snug shorts. "Well, I'm not." April watched for some sign of remorse or vulnerability or at least anger to cross Wil's slightly freckled face, but instead she *smiled*.

April turned angrily, walking purposefully across the lawn to the Lodge—and as far away from her new roommate as she could get.

# CHAPTER 5

**DATE:** June 29th

**FOOD:** ½ apple with ¼ c. yogurt and 1 bottle Vitamin Water

**EXERCISE:** Power-walking away from my roommate

THE WELLNESS CANYON INITIATION WAS A THREE-PART PROCESS: snapping a "before" shot for the Wellness Canyon yearbook, standing for a head-to-toe measurement to determine body-fat distribution and body mass index, and finally, a series of individual fitness tests to measure heart rate, flexibility, and overall strength. April glanced at Wil, who had followed her to the Lodge despite April's attempt to get away from her. Now Wil was humming some repetitive song by a lame group that she probably thought was "indie." April rolled her eyes, hoping she didn't need her roommate for anything yet.

The afternoon sun cast dark shadows along the front of the Lodge and April imagined a burly mountain man standing on the porch, trying to find her in the crowd. Her mom read almost exclusively thick romance novels, the kind with pictures of long-haired maidens on the front, fainting into the arms of the strong and handsome hero. Even though April made fun of her for them—everyone knew they didn't count as real books—she wasn't above stealing one away to her room once in a while and flipping through to the exciting parts. It was all the romance she was going to get, after all. Except—she'd kind of hoped Wellness Canyon would also be an answer to her lackluster love life. Everyone here was in the same boat as she was, right? That meant her chances had to be at least a little better than they were out there, in the real world.

An older man in a white lab coat and thick black glasses stood under the porch of the wooden building, a clipboard held tightly to his chest. He smiled when Melanie and Kevin approached. "Everyone, this is Dr. Hausler," Melanie announced into the crowd of lingering campers.

"House!" some of the campers called out in unison.

"Hey, guys!" Dr. Hausler said, laughing at the nickname. "Good to see you back!"

"Split in half—but stay with your roommates—half go with Dr. Hausler for measurements and half line up at the other end of the porch for 'before' pictures," Melanie directed, her red hair bobbing as she motioned to an invisible line where the crowd should split.

The crowd parted magically down the middle at Melanie's request, and April and Wil found themselves waiting for photos. Kevin kept the line moving quickly, directing each camper to their mark in front of the wooden wall while another counselor snapped the pictures with a digital camera.

"Next!" Kevin reached for April as he positioned her in against the wall. His grip was surprisingly strong and April was embarrassed by the amount of flesh he held while holding her arm. She smiled sweetly for the camera and made little adjustments, hoping for the best possible picture. She elongated her neck to minimize the roll underneath and sucked everything in just before the flash went off.

"Next," Kevin said again, nodding that April should head to Dr. Hausler and reaching for Wil in one motion. Wil brushed off Kevin's hand and leaned against the wall, her arms squeezed against her sides, which everyone knew was unflattering.

"Ready, set, go," the counselor behind the camera said, and Wil stuck out her tongue just as the camera whirred and clicked. The counselor didn't seem to notice and Kevin called out for the next camper to step up.

Dr. Hausler's hands fluttered around April's body like butterflies. He pulled a cloth tape measure tight and then released it, calling out the measurements to Melanie, who recorded them in a BlackBerry. Then April went up the stairs and got onto one of the giant scales they'd pulled out onto the porch. She watched the balance sway and finally settle on a number higher than April ever remembered it being before: 205. April was momentarily depressed but then repeated the number to herself in order to memorize it. *That* would be the "before."

Next, she went back into the shade of the building and sweated through the jumping jacks and learned that her heart rate—though not ideal—was normal for someone of her size.

She managed three push-ups and completed the toe touch, although she had to bend her knees for the final few inches. April was a little embarrassed at her results, but just kept telling herself that it would just make it all the more exciting when they did their final tests at the end of the summer. She vowed to amaze the counselors and Dr. Hausler.

The last fitness test required roommates to pair up, one holding the ankles of the other while counting the number of crunches they could do in two minutes. Half of the campers tumbled to the grass and stared up at the blue sky as they folded their fingers behind their heads. Next to April and Wil, Colin and his redheaded roommate were settling in. On their other side, Jessica lay down on the grass while her roommate got into place at her feet.

April felt Wil grab her ankles a little too strongly. "Ready?" April asked.

"I was born ready," Wil replied dryly, tightening her grip.

April tensed her stomach in anticipation of the coming pain.

"Anytime," Wil offered, glancing at her watch.

With Colin this close, April felt a little thrill run through her veins. She quickly hoisted herself up, her arms flapping in a burst of momentum.

"One," Wil deadpanned. A patch of clouds temporarily blocked out the sun and for a moment it looked like it might rain.

"Two."

The clouds passed and the lawn was lit again in brilliant

sunlight. April continued to force her body up off the ground, a symphony of pain in her neck, stomach, back, and arms joining in a whole concert of agony. She couldn't tell if the awful grunting noise was in her mind or if she was actually making it. She hoped it was the former.

"Six."

April swore it was seven, not six, but couldn't find the breath to complain. She just tried to keep moving because she knew that once she rested her shoulders on the scratchy green grass, it would all be over. She turned her eyes to the left slightly and saw Colin finishing a set of rapid crunches.

"How many have you done?" April heard Jessica ask Colin teasingly as she continued at her own quick pace.

Colin wiped the sweat from his forehead. "Fifty-seven," he panted, and continued his rapid sit-ups, smiling over at Jessica on his other side.

"Nine," Wil muttered to April. April felt her knees begin to drift apart, her thighs shaking uncontrollably. She kept forcing herself to do sit-ups, but she was going much slower now. The muscles in her stomach were so cramped that she could hardly move. She took a break for a second, letting her shoulder blades rest against the grass, and heard whispering.

"So, you up for tonight?" Jessica asked Colin, lowering her voice to an almost-inaudible level.

"Absolutely, babe." Colin nodded, pushing himself into another sit-up. He wiped the sweat off his face with his T-shirt before continuing.

"After lights-out," Jessica said, looking around suspiciously. Her gaze fell on April and she smiled at Jessica, trying to convey that she wouldn't expose their secret plans. Jessica smiled back at her, but it was a vacant, throwaway smile. "Meet me at the place I told you," Jessica said before turning back to her partner.

"Eleven," Wil said. "Come on, April. You still have thirty seconds."

April lay back against the grass, deflated. The sweet smell of the lawn permeated April's nose, and she could feel the individual blades stickily clinging to the backs of her arms and legs.

"Is that it?" Wil poked her on the ankle.

April didn't answer. Was she that invisible? Her whole life she'd prayed for people not to see her, but she thought for sure things would be different at Wellness Canyon. She *wanted* to be seen here, wanted to be included, wouldn't be afraid that an invitation would end up as a joke at her expense, but she'd been here for hours already and no one even knew who she was besides her bitter, nasty roommate.

"Hey," Wil asked again, "is that it?"

"Huh? Oh, uh . . ." April began. She shook as she struggled to get in one last sit-up.

"Okay, switch!" Kevin called out to the group doing sit-ups. "Record your results in your notebooks and we'll come around to get your numbers at the end." All around April, campers busily started jotting things down.

Wil grunted and got into place on the ground. April grabbed Wil's ankles through her jeans and waited for Kevin to start them. "You know, if you hadn't been so obsessed with watching certain people," she said significantly, looking over toward Colin and Jessica, "you might have actually been able to do a good number of sit-ups."

"Oh, please. Like you can do better," April replied, annoyed that Wil had noticed her eavesdropping on Jessica and Colin's conversation.

"Better than you," Wil said confidently, her eyes squinted in the sunlight.

April squeezed Wil's ankles in response. She smiled when she saw Wil wince slightly. April's legs itched from the dry grass on the lawn, but she didn't reach to scratch. She was having too much fun torturing Wil.

"Ready?" Kevin looked out over the campers spread out on the lawn. "And go!"

"C'mon, Wil," April said, glaring at Wil as she started her sit-ups. "Prove it."

# CHAPTER 6

**DATE:** June 30th

**FOOD:** 1 c. oatmeal with ½ cup fresh raspberries, 0 apple pancakes

**EXERCISE:** Tons of push-ups—well, only 7, but my knees weren't touching!—and 11 sit-ups

"GUESS WE SHOULD'VE GOTTEN HERE EARLIER," APRIL SAID, HER voice tinged with accusation as she slammed her breakfast tray down on the long wooden table and looked at her depressing little bowl of Kashi oatmeal. She'd tried to spruce it up with raspberries, but the raspberries had melted into tiny red splotches. Then she shot a look at Wil, who had sat down across from her with a tray carrying only a single white mug filled with black coffee and about eight packets of Splenda.

April looked longingly over at the group of laughing campers at the table next to her, their plates heaping with the camp's delicious-looking whole-wheat-and-flax pancakes with baked apples and cinnamon. After sleeping through two alarms, Wil had spent half an hour in the shower while April waited patiently at the foot of her made bed, dressed and ready for breakfast. She hadn't said anything when Wil sauntered out of the shower, her towel barely covering her body. She hadn't said anything when she waited another ten minutes for Wil to slowly get dressed. And she hadn't said anything as she and Wil ambled over to Dickinson—the hall that served as the dining hall but could also be converted for lectures, concerts, and parties.

But now she couldn't hold it in anymore. They were stuck sitting at a table in the back of the palatial, airy building; they'd missed getting pancakes; and they were rushing through breakfast so they wouldn't be late for the first activity of the day.

April took a deep breath but couldn't think of anything good to say to Wil. "You know," April said finally. "You should really eat something." April was positively starving and couldn't fathom how or why Wil was going to try to get by on a cup of coffee. "You might pass out."

"Oh, thanks for the tip, *Mom*. I think I'll be okay," Wil said sarcastically. She rolled her eyes and took a huge sip of her coffee for emphasis.

"Attention, everyone!" The microphone squealed during Melanie's announcement, and Kevin quickly hurried to her side to fool around with some of the buttons. The echo chased around the large, high-ceilinged room, past all the floor-to-ceiling murals against the far wall, down and around the large fish tank in the far corner. April glanced at Wil, who was leaning back in her chair, arms crossed against her chest. April rolled her eyes.

The microphone squawked once again and April inadvertently put her hands over her ears. Finally Kevin tapped the mic and handed it back to Melanie, who said, "I'd like to announce the teams now." The room quieted immediately.

April turned her chair around to face the front of the dining hall, happy not to be facing Wil, who had started tapping her sneaker against the table leg irritatingly.

"We took a lot of factors into consideration when we drew up these teams," Melanie said excitedly. "Even though Kevin wanted to just put your names into a hat." The lame joke caught Kevin off guard and he bowed ceremoniously as a smatter of mock boos was directed at him. "So, please pay attention," Melanie said. "When your team is called, please raise your hands so you can all find each other."

April crossed her fingers in her lap and listened to the roster of names read over the speakers. A quartet of hands shot into the air and each newly minted team drew up chairs at one of the empty tables. *Please, please, please let me be on Colin's team. Or Jessica's. Anyone but Wil.* Four more names were read, and one of the girls let out a shriek of excitement and then hugged her new teammates.

"Oh, gross," Wil said, rolling her eyes.

April glared at her.

"Jessica Hart and Marci Tannenbaum," Melanie read from her list. April squeezed her fingers together tightly. *Please, please, please.* She silently vowed to give up ice cream forever if she could just be on their team. "And Colin Brady and Gregg

Drakapoulous." April's shoulders drooped as Colin and his roommate, Gregg, high-fived. Jessica and Marci wound their way across the room to the boys' table. Jessica tucked her hair behind her ears as she sat down and April watched as Marci did the same. She snuck a look at Wil, who seemed to be sleeping in her chair. Then April tentatively raised a hand to her head and tucked one side of her hair behind her ear too.

"April Adams and Wilhelmina Hopkins," Melanie called out. Wil managed to wake from her faux slumber to cringe. "And Dave Rossdale and Paul Archer."

April raised her hand in the air and looked around for the others. "Raise your hand," April whispered to Wil, who plopped her elbow on the table and raised a limp hand.

"Paul's a fat kid's name if I ever heard one," Wil scoffed.

And indeed, a very chubby boy, in khaki shorts and a T-shirt that read PAUL'S FISH-AND-CHIPS over a British flag, lumbered toward April and Wil, running his fingers nervously across his dark crew cut with one hand and holding a crowded tray with the other.

"Ahoy, Paul," Wil said. She saluted him and kicked out a chair in a welcome gesture.

"Uh, I'm David. Well, Dave," the boy said nervously as he backed into the empty chair. "I know my shirt says Paul's, but we just thought it would be a funny joke. Um, ha ha." He pulled his shirt away from his stomach and scooted up to the table. "Paul's still in line for his food. They . . . uh . . . put out another batch of pancakes."

April glanced back at the food area. There was another long line forming, but now that she had a little bowl of oatmeal, she couldn't go back. Seconds were too embarrassing.

"I'm April," she introduced herself. "And this is Wil."

Wil stuck out her hand and Dave shook it. "Strong grip." Wil nodded in approval and threw back her shoulders as if she was impressed. "That bodes well for our team's chances of winning the gold," Wil muttered sarcastically.

Dave smiled nervously, looking like he wasn't sure if she was making a joke at his expense or not. April had felt that way so many times herself already and smiled at him reassuringly.

"So, uh, where are you guys from?" Dave asked, cutting into his pancakes with his knife and fork.

"San Luis Obispo," April replied. Watching Dave eat the pancakes suddenly reminded April of the breakfast spread that her mom had made the day she left. Just thinking about it made her feel glad to be here, away from everything. "Where are you from?"

"Phoenix," Dave said, flicking a crumb across the table with his forefinger.

"Cool!" April said, leaning in closer. "I've always wanted to go to Arizona."

Dave shrugged his immense shoulders. "The summers are too hot." He smiled at April before he turned to Wil. "What about you?" he asked her.

"Malibu," Wil said, taking a small sip of her black coffee and grimacing. She grabbed a yellow Splenda packet off her tray and twisted it with her fingers until it burst, sending little white flecks all over April, the table, and the floor. Wil snickered. "Whoops."

"Ugh!" April grunted, brushing herself off. "Wil—," she started.

"What?" Wil laughed. "A little sugar substitute going to hurt you?" she asked in a mocking voice.

In the distance, April saw Jessica, Marci, Colin, and Gregg huddled around their table like a bunch of heads of state, making plans to invade. Colin was drawing something on a napkin. Suddenly a boy nearly twice Dave's size waddled in front of April. He was swaddled in a black sweat suit, his greasy, dirty blond hair sticking up in peaks.

"Hey," the boy said as he lowered his body into his seat, his pancake-filled tray clattering against the table. "I'm Paul." He reached across the table for a napkin and sent the saltshaker tumbling to the floor near April's foot, but she pretended not to notice. Her stomach ached from the dozen sit-ups she'd managed the day before, and there was no way she could bend over to retrieve it. The smell of hot apples rose from the table.

"So," Paul said between bites. "Where are y'all from?" April stared at his pancakes with envy. "I'm from Modesto. Northern California."

"That's a bad scene," Wil said, whistling softly. "A friend of mine was mugged in Modesto. She was there visiting her grandmother or something and she went out for, like, a walk and that's when they got her. Broad daylight, too."

Paul slowed his chewing and eyed Wil, as if trying to solve a puzzle. "I don't remember hearing about that."

"It was all over the news." Wil shrugged. "Anyway"—she glanced at Paul with a sarcastic look—"glad *you* made it out alive." Wil swung her mug at him and took a sip.

"Have you ever even *been* to Modesto?" April asked, dropping her spoon into her bowl. She couldn't believe she would be stuck with Wil for the *whole* summer.

"Me?" Wil asked, her blue eyes wide with incredulity. "Honey, this is as far north of L.A. as I go. I get nosebleeds anywhere above Bakersfield." April stared at Wil, seething, before picking her spoon back up and taking another bite of her oatmeal. She turned away from the bright morning sunlight streaming through the floor-to-ceiling windows across from their table.

"So . . . uh . . . where in L.A. do you live?" Dave asked tentatively, sharing a glance with Paul. Great. Wil was going to make their teammates hate them. April braced for another foul wind from Wil's mouth.

"Only vapid idiots live in L.A." Wil laughed, tapping her chipped black nails against the table. "I live in Malibu. Maybe you've seen it on TV."

Everyone sat in awkward silence as the din from the other groups washed over them. Wil slumped back down in her chair as April shielded her eyes from the sun and glanced longingly at Jessica's table, where Marci and Gregg were arm-wrestling. Jessica clamped down on their wrists with both hands in a vain attempt to pull their arms toward Marci's side and April sighed. She had no idea what she had done to get stuck with someone like Wil for the summer.

"Keep dreaming. You're stuck with us," Wil said to April, smiling as she stood up. Then Wil sauntered out of the airy cafeteria, leaving her empty mug and tray filled with empty Splenda packets behind.

April sighed again and then turned back to her team-mates. She shrugged. And then Paul hooted. "Oh yeah, this team's gonna be *awesome*."

# CHAPTER 7

**DATE:** June 30th

**FOOD:** 1 cup coffee, 1 Splenda packet, and half a shampoo bottle of M&Ms

**EXERCISE:** As if. I only did the initiation exercises to get that psycho-Barbie Melanie to leave me alone.

"OKAY! EVERYONE KNOWS WHAT A TRUST TUMBLE IS, RIGHT?" Melanie called out from the center of the lawn. A murmur floated across the damp grass like a fog. Wil felt like tearing out her hair. Maybe plucking it out, one strand at a time. She couldn't believe that it was only the first full day here. It was like freaking torture.

Melanie turned to Kevin, who was, as usual, practically on top of her, and the other counselors. "Did you hear something?"

Kevin shrugged and looked comically over his shoulder, as if to see if there was anyone around. The two of them were totally doing it. No way would he be her whipping boy like that without getting something in return.

"I can't hear you!" Melanie shouted.

"Yes!" the crowd roared, except for Wil, who shouted, "No!" at the top of her lungs, drowned out by the sheep surrounding her. Her stomach growled, but there was no way in hell she was going to admit to being hungry, especially after watching that large dorkus Paul suck down his second helping of pancakes. With his hair sticking up and his huge stomach sticking out, Paul was a dead ringer for SpongeBob's fat friend, Patrick. Wil snickered and then she sighed as she looked around her. On each side of her were eager campers, ready to do anything Melanie said and ready to try whatever idiotic weight-loss technique the camp would throw at them—despite the fact that all of them had most likely tried everything already and this was some lame, overpriced last-ditch effort.

Unlike them, all *Wil* really wanted was a one-way ticket out of Loserville and back to the real world. And if she had to spend the entire summer tethered to her obviously popularity-obsessed roommate, she knew she would go insane.

"If we can't learn to trust each other, then all is lost." Melanie droned on like an inspirational talk show host. She was more like a cartoon character than a real person, and each time she spoke, Wil half expected her words to appear above her head in a white bubble. "So it's important that we *start out* knowing that we can trust each other. Not just trust between roommates, but trust within your team, too. Your success this summer depends on it." She turned to Kevin. "We're going to perform trust tumbles as a team to symbolize team trust. Here's a demonstration. Ready?"

"Ready!" Kevin said enthusiastically, his perfect blond hair not budging as he nodded. He'd probably been waiting all day for the chance to grope Melanie.

Melanie turned her back to Kevin and planted her feet. Kevin inched forward, shuffling into position.

"Pervert." Wil snickered, louder than she'd intended. Dave and Paul laughed, as did the other campers within earshot. The distraction caught Melanie's eye and she froze, casting a glance in Wil's direction.

"Okay," Melanie said. "To show how much I trust Kevin, I'm going to close my eyes and tumble backward, knowing that Kevin isn't going to let me fall." Melanie crossed her arms across her chest dramatically and closed her eyes. She fell convincingly backward, landing squarely in Kevin's arms.

"Can we keep what we catch?" a tall, stocky boy asked, and everyone laughed.

Wil smirked and glanced at the boy who spoke—she'd seen him stand up during the team assignments but hadn't been paying attention. She vaguely remembered the blond girl that April was obsessed with—Jessica—calling him Colin. The idea that there might be someone half cool at Wellness Canyon hadn't even crossed her mind.

"Catch and release," Kevin said. He set Melanie back upright.

"Kevin and I will come around and match up the teams into larger groups. Everyone in the group *must* catch everyone else at least once. You can continue to go around the circle as many times as you want. Something good can be done better and better until it's your best: good, better, best!"

"Sad, sadder, *sadist*," Wil said, loud enough for Colin to hear. He smiled at her.

"Excuse me?" Melanie and the others stared at her.

"Nothing." Wil smiled innocently, putting an I'm-really-really-excited-to-be-here look on her face.

Melanie finally turned away from Wil, satisfied, and focused her attention on breaking the campers into groups of two teams each. She walked through the crowd, tapping people on the shoulder with her quick-moving hands and making them form large circles. Kevin spread out in the opposite direction and wrangled Wil, April, Paul, and Dave into a circle with Jessica, Marci, Gregg, and Colin. Wil tried to catch Colin's eye and give him a this-sucks smirk, but he was too busy flirting with Jessica and Marci while Gregg looked on admiringly.

Paul moved in behind Wil while the others paired up.

"What are you doing?" Wil turned toward him crankily. She could feel her body beginning to overheat in her black T-shirt. It wasn't exactly a good sign if just standing in the sun doing *nothing* could exhaust her.

"Fall and I'll catch you," Paul said confidently, holding his enormous arms out in front of him. His messy blond hair fell in front of his eyes and he blew it away, making him look like an enormous puffer fish.

Wil eyed him warily and laughed. "No thanks."

"But you have to," Paul protested. "Everyone has to do it at least once."

Wil stared at Colin across the circle as Jessica fell, giggling, into his arms. She glanced back at Paul and examined him critically. She could see herself knocking him over with her fall, the two of them tumbling over on the grass as if they were part of some comic sumo-wrestling skit. No way was she going to rely on Paul from Modesto to save her from public humiliation.

Though maybe if Colin offered to catch her, she would have reconsidered.

"It's easy," Dave spoke up. He smiled reassuringly at Wil. "Watch." He closed his eyes and let his body fall backward. April caught his shoulders before he fell very far. He stood up again and flashed a grin at April, winking. "See."

"All *I* see is an accident waiting to happen." Wil wrinkled her nose in distaste.

"Would you just try, Wil?" April huffed, putting her hands on her ample hips.

Wil smiled tightly. "No, I'll leave that to you," she said in a sweet, sarcastic voice. "That way, you can take my turn and catch Jessica twice. I mean, since you're always staring at her, I figured you wouldn't mind."

April's jaw dropped open and she flushed bright red. Wil smirked, knowing that she had hit a sore spot. April stared into Wil's eyes, visibly grinding her jaw before she turned to Paul. "C'mon. Ready?"

50

"Ready!" Paul said, getting into place in front of April. He fell neatly into April's arms and April caught his shoulders.

Wil laughed. "Almost dropped that one, April! Better tr—"

"Wilhelmina, will you step over here for a minute?" Melanie demanded in her cheerful but no-nonsense voice. When Wil looked into her icy blue eyes, it wasn't hard to guess that Melanie wasn't pulling her aside for a friendly chat.

Wil felt everyone's eyes on her back as Melanie led her up the wide wooden steps to the porch of the Lodge. Wil caught Colin's attention so he could witness her long eye roll. Then she looked back at April and smirked.

Suddenly, a loud thud broke the silence. Everyone stopped staring at Wil and looked into the circle where her former teammates stood. Wil stifled a laugh as Dave hit the ground, bracing his fall with a wayward elbow while Paul just stood there redfaced. "Moron," Dave said, looking up at Paul.

"I *told* you so," Wil called out before Melanie yanked her out of earshot.

Inside her office in the Lodge, Melanie told Wil to sit. Wil sat down in a chair with a little purple embroidered pillow on it that said THINK BEFORE YOU EAT. Apparently, Melanie was really into motivational sayings. On the wall opposite her, Melanie's old jeans that she had shown at orientation hung on a hook next to a framed before/after shot that Wil assumed was Melanie, pre–weight loss.

"Wilhelmina, I'll keep this short," Melanie began, pushing her small iBook to the side of her desk.

"It's just Wil," Wil corrected her, cringing.

"I'm giving you a demerit for your behavior on the lawn today," Melanie reprimanded.

"Oh no!" Wil said, feigning horror. She rolled her eyes. She wondered how many demerits it took to get kicked out of Wellness Canyon altogether. She hoped the number was incredibly low.

"Look." Melanie crossed her arms on her desk and peered over at Wil. "I don't know what your problem is. All I know is that you need to shape up or this whole summer is going to be wasted. I know it's hard to live with new people and to be away from your friends for the summer, but Wilhelmina, you have to keep your eyes on the prize." Melanie sat back and placed her hands in her lap just like Wil's shrink back home did. She looked incredibly pleased with herself.

"Kiss my butt," Wil muttered. Then she bolted up so fast that she nearly tipped the chair over. She looked at Melanie for one long moment and then turned to leave.

"That's another demerit, Wil!" Melanie called after her, probably thinking it would just break Wil apart to be so close to being kicked out.

But truthfully, it was exactly what Wil had wanted. She kept herself looking straight ahead so Melanie wouldn't catch the huge grin plastered across her face.

# CHAPTER 8

**DATE:** July 4th
**FOOD:** 1 c. steamed broccoli with salt and pepper, ½ c. whole-wheat couscous, and 1 grilled chicken breast (I was careful to make sure it wasn't larger than my fist)
**EXERCISE:** A full 60-minute circuit with my trainer. He said I'm doing great!

APRIL WAS IN DICKINSON FINISHING UP HER DINNER WITH DAVE and Paul when she looked up and saw Melanie approaching with a big smile on her face. "Hi Melanie!" she squeaked, carefully displaying the remnants of her extremely healthy meal.

"Great workout yesterday, Dave," Melanie said, placing her small hand on Dave's ample shoulder. "And April, I wanted to let you know that you have a package. It's in your mailbox in the Lodge. You can pick it up whenever."

"Thanks! Do you know who it's from?" April asked, sitting up a little straighter. She grinned at Paul and Dave.

"Nope, but it's a big one," Melanie said lightly. "Enjoy free time tonight, guys, and happy Fourth of July!" She bustled away from their table, stopping only to pick up a stray napkin off the ground and then to yell at Colin and Gregg when they started flinging pieces of broccoli off of their forks.

April stood up from the squishy Wellness Canyon logo–embroidered dining chair and gathered her things. "What are you up to tonight?" she asked Dave and Paul as she picked up her tray.

"I don't know—probably just hanging out. Dave brought some board games and we're in the middle of a serious game of Risk right now," Paul said, pretending to glare at Dave as the three of them headed to the window to bus their trays.

"Dude, I'm *so* taking Australia from you tonight," Dave threatened Paul, chucking his silverware down the chute. Then Dave turned to April and leaned in as if to tell her a secret. "He sucks at Risk." He winked at her.

April giggled and put her tray and silverware away. She then said goodbye to the guys and checked the bulletin board quickly to see if there was anything going on that night—just the fireworks—and headed out of the dining hall and over to the Lodge.

April smiled as she started down the pebbled trail toward the center of camp. Wellness Canyon was so peaceful this time of night. Most of the campers were still in the dining hall, and those who were out seemed to be looking for a little bit of peace at the end of the busy day. Out on the misty lake, April could just barely see a loon glide onto the water and dive for its dinner. The night was breezy and cool, but little ankle-height lanterns were coming on and they lit the path in front of her. Wellness Canyon was a lot of work—and crazy expensive—but it was so beautiful. *Oh yeah,* April thought. *This was totally worth it.*

She sped up a little, past the spa building, up the wide steps of the Lodge and through the open doors. April walked down the hallway, and past the large lounge, which featured a custom-made pool table with the Wellness Canyon logo on it, a dartboard, and a Pirates of the Caribbean pinball table with a huge picture of Jack Sparrow. Plush leather couches sat in front of a huge plasma television hanging on the wall. On the opposite side of the room was a smoothie and frozen yogurt bar where some campers were already lining up for their July Fourth–themed dessert—raspberry, blueberry, and plain yogurt parfaits. The huge windowed room also held the communal camp phone. Most campers had cell phones, but the phone was still there for anyone who might need to use it—like April.

She continued on to the little mail office at the end of the hallway. Even though she knew the package had to be from her mom, she was really excited. Maybe she'd even sent her some new workout clothes! She'd thought hers would be adequate—at least they were new—but after seeing what nice, fancy things everyone else had, all of her stuff felt so shabby.

April went up to the desk and rang the bell for help. A young, kind of cute guy that April didn't recognize poked his head out of an office. He definitely wasn't a camper. "Oh, hey," he said to April, as he finished chewing something. "Name?" he asked.

"April Adams. Melanie told me that I have a package," she explained, twirling her ponytail around in her fingers.

"Just a second." The guy walked back into the office and returned a few seconds later with a large box and put it up on the counter for April. "Here you go. Enjoy!" he said and then bounced back into the office.

April grabbed the box and excitedly looked around for a place where she could open it. There wasn't even a chair in the hallway, so she walked back down to the lounge and plopped down onto one of the large couches. Behind her, a few kids were starting a rousing game of pool.

She reached into her pocket and pulled out her keys to cut through the tape on the top of the box. As she did, she saw that her mom had decorated the "to" label with sparkly little star stickers, and even though she was a little embarrassed, April smiled. She gingerly opened the box and removed some glittery tissue paper. Maybe her mom had sent her T-shirts! Or new underwear! Or even better, some money for tips so that she could send her laundry out like the other campers did.

At the bottom of the cardboard box April found a metal tin. She excitedly removed the lid with a flourish. Inside were what must have been about three dozen of her mother's home-made peanut butter chocolate chip delight bars. On top of those was a note that said, *I'm so proud of you!* in her mother's pretty cursive.

April just stared at the peanut butter chocolate chip delight bars in horror, unable to move. Around her, the Lodge lounge was buzzing with campers. The pool game was in full swing, and several other kids were watching, eating their red, white, and blue yogurt desserts and chatting. Another group was playing Monopoly and half-watching reruns of Degrassi on the TV. But April just stared at the box, unable to fathom why her mother would ever have thought that sending cookies to her daughter at a *weight-loss spa* would be a good idea.

Tears stung her eyes and April looked around, longing for someone to talk to, to confide in. But when she looked up, no one was looking at her. In fact, nobody even seemed to notice that she was even sitting there on the couch at all.

"Hey, cookies!" she heard behind her and turned to see Colin. Then he reached over her and grabbed a bar out of the tin. April felt herself blush, but before she had a chance to explain that *of course* she wouldn't be eating the cookies, that her mom had sent them, and if he liked them so much, he could just go ahead and have them, he was already halfway across the room, with Jessica, Marci, and Gregg at his side.

April gathered the box and tissue paper and got up off the couch. She could feel that she was going to cry, and if she had no one to talk to at the Lodge, then she'd rather just be by herself. April hurried toward the exit, stopping only to throw the care package in the large garbage can by the double doors. She didn't let herself cry until she reached the dark lawn. She collapsed onto the ground at the base of a tree, the cool Wellness Canyon breeze swirling around her lone, sobbing figure.

# CHAPTER 9

**DATE:** July 8th

**FOOD:** ½ bottle Power-C Vitamin Water,
1 helping no-oil chicken-and-veggie
stir-fry over ½ c. steamed brown rice.
I feel skinnier already! Possible?

**EXERCISE:** I've been working on sit-ups. Up to 25
already!

A FEW DAYS LATER, ALL OF THE WELLNESS CANYON CAMPERS
were supposed to power-walk down the one-mile driveway, out
the main gates, across Wellness Canyon Drive—which divided
the town into its north and south neighborhoods—and through
a wooded trail that circled back into camp past Lake Jennings.
The whole circuit was about five miles.

"I'm not too sure about the wooded-trail part of this
whole thing," Wil complained, already breathing a little heavier.
"The only good thing that can come out of *that* is a case of
Lyme disease."

April rolled her eyes and kept walking. After getting the

"care package" from her mom a few days ago, April had vowed to work even harder than before. If her mom didn't understand what this meant to her, then it really was up to her—and her alone—to make it work. And besides, she was determined not to let Wil get to her on such a glorious, sunny day.

"Anyway, this whole thing is so stupid. I can't stand people at my school in Malibu, so why would it be any different here? They're all loaded and entitled and just so...vapid. I mean, all of our parents paid like seven grand for their precious little fatties to go away and come back pretty and normal. I just hate it," Wil complained.

Listening to Wil, April felt like an imposter. She was the one who'd paid seven grand to go away and come back pretty and normal.

"Wil, why are you always so negative?" April asked, swatting at a fly. She replayed Wil's obnoxiousness in the dining hall from a few days ago in her mind.

"I'm not negative," Wil responded flatly, clearly not taking offense. She walked slowly, barely lifting her black Converse low-tops off the ground. "I'm just telling the truth."

April noticed that she and Wil were lagging behind the other campers and took a full stride forward to catch up. There was no *way* that they would burn enough calories at this pace. "Well, 'telling the truth' is rubbing off on everyone else and bringing all of us down with you." April spotted Jessica's ponytail tucked into a Boston Red Sox hat far in front of the pack and picked up the pace some more, hoping to catch up and join them.

"Hey, let's slow it down," Wil called, ten feet behind. "This ain't a race." Wil coughed and spit in the direction of the wrought-iron gates.

April sighed dramatically and waited for Wil to catch up, knowing that she would get in trouble with Melanie if she took off without her roommate. They'd reached the street, and April looked both ways, waiting for the cars to pass so they could cross. But the traffic never seemed to end, and April saw the group in front of them getting farther and farther ahead. April flinched when a red Ford pickup truck let out two short honks as it breezed by.

They finally crossed the road and slipped down the wooded trail. April could just make out Paul's shirt through the trees and cactus.

"Who are you looking for?" Wil asked. April could feel Wil's eyes watching her.

"What? Nobody."

"Afraid Jessica is going to get too far away?"

April glared at her roommate and stepped over a root in the middle of the trail. If Wil had been a decent person, April would have given her a warning about it, but she wasn't, so April didn't. Wil easily stepped over it anyway. "No. I'm just trying not to fall too far behind," April said firmly.

"Jessica doesn't even belong here, you know," Wil continued. She panted a little and hiked up her black shorts, fanning off her legs in the process. "If she dropped ten pounds, they probably wouldn't even let her stay. Hey, do you think she has . . . you know . . . food *issues*?"

"What are you even talking about?" April asked, exasperated. "You don't even *know* Jessica and Marci. They seem really nice." The woods were so pretty and peaceful, and if she could just walk along quietly, she'd be able to enjoy the sense of accomplishment that came from actually doing something challenging. April felt beads of sweat trickling down her thighs. She continued. "I mean, what if Jessica was saying all these things about *you*?"

"Well, you'd probably join in the fun, right?" Wil paused and crouched down to retie her shoe.

April paused and saw the last of the crowd in front of them disappear around a bend. She sighed deeply, staring up at the blue sky. There was no way April could last until August as Wil's roommate. She would have given up all her sugar-free chocolate mousse desserts for the rest of the summer to be Jessica's roommate, or Marci's, or *anyone* at all who wanted to be at Wellness Canyon and didn't bring everything and everyone around her down.

Wil stood up and the two of them walked on in silence, April trying to not let Wil get to her. With each step, she tried to think of the calories that were burning up and disappearing into the atmosphere. She repeated the mantra that Melanie had taught them in her head as she took each step. *Fit not fat. Fit not fat.* April smiled to herself.

Wil suddenly stopped in the middle of the trail and looked both ways. "Hey, do you have any idea where we are?"

April shook herself out of her daze and jogged a few yards, squinting ahead, but no one was in sight. No bright, sweat-soaked

T-shirts on oversized bodies, no giggles, jokes, or complaints. It looked like the two of them had somehow managed to wander off the well-worn trail onto some kind of smaller trail, this one patchy and sandy and lined with low scrub brush. She shielded her eyes against the sun. "Great," she moaned to Wil. "You got us lost!"

"*I* got us lost?" Wil asked, scratching at a bug bite on the underside of her flabby, tanned arm. "I thought you knew where you were going."

"How would *I* know where we were going?" April shouted, exasperated. She felt like screaming as loud as she could. Maybe someone would come to save her from her roommate. "We were just supposed to follow the others. *I* was *trying* to follow the others." She glared at Wil accusingly. "But you can't even do that."

"Moron," Wil muttered under her breath.

April whirled around. "What did you say?"

Wil backed up a step and just stared at April.

"What did you say?" April asked again. She couldn't *believe* she had gotten stuck with a roommate like Wil. And that Melanie had paired them together on *purpose*. It was unfathomable.

"Hey, wait. What's that over there?" Wil nodded her curly head toward something off to the right that looked like an opening in a dense thicket. "Maybe that's the way." April followed silently as Wil led them up a small hill and through the opening at the top. Wil held a thorny hedge so that April could duck underneath. Well, that was kind of a nice, roommatey thing for her to do. April felt a little bad about wishing she'd tripped on the root earlier.

When they got through, April sucked in her breath. Much of the hike had been uphill and they were now overlooking a small valley past which April could just barely make out Santa Barbara and the radiant blue of the Pacific Ocean.

"Oh, hell, yes," Wil said. She whistled.

April smiled over at Wil. "I know, isn't it beauti—" and then she stopped when she saw that Wil was not, in fact, looking at the view, but at something much closer instead: a 7-Eleven at the bottom of the hill.

# CHAPTER 10

**DATE:** July 8th

**FOOD:** Some crappy coffee with way too much Splenda to make up for the lack of sugar in my diet. And I'm starving.

**EXERCISE:** All of this walking is really starting to annoy me. . . .

WIL PUSHED OPEN THE DOUBLE DOORS TO THE 7-ELEVEN, holding them open for April. The air-conditioning rushed at her and dried her sweat. Under the fluorescent lighting, the store gleamed. Even though it had only been ten days, Wil felt like she'd crawled through the hot desert for weeks and stumbled into an oasis of candy, pastry, and potato chips. She rounded the Little Debbie display, April on her heels. Everything looked so colorful and beautiful that she thought she would cry. "I'm starving," Wil admitted as she started down the candy aisle.

"Isn't this cheating?" April asked, looking around nervously. Her soft brown eyes swept across the brightly colored packages of delicious goodness.

"Oh, please. C'mon—what's your favorite?" Wil asked in a slow, dazed voice, totally ignoring April. "My stranded-on-a-desert-island top five candies are, in no particular order, Twix, Snickers, Peppermint Patties, Take 5, and Nestlé Crunch. Well, that's not including Jacques Torres and Godiva, of course."

"Well, I *love* Hershey's Kisses," April said, touching a shiny bag filled with the little foil pyramids.

"But that's so boring. . . . They're just little lumps of chocolate." Wil almost felt bad for April. That was kind of sad, Hershey's Kisses being her favorite candy. They were the kind of candy in the reception area of her shrink's—the kind she never bothered to take.

"Some have nuts," April muttered, looking hurt. She moved down the aisle, flipping over the packages to look at the nutrition tables.

Wil snatched a Twix. "Hey, watch this," she said. She put her hand over a Snickers bar and made it disappear into her sleeve. "Pretty cool, eh?"

"Wil," April whispered, looking panicked. Her brown eyes were wide with fear, just like they had been when they'd thought they were lost. "We'll get caught!"

"No, we won't," Wil shot back. She didn't know whether she would eat her Twix first or the Snickers. "I do it all the time."

"You are so busted!" a loud male voice said behind them. They whirled around and April dropped a bag of gummi bears. But instead of a green-smocked 7-Eleven employee, Colin stood in front of them laughing. He was wearing a USC T-shirt with coordinating mesh shorts.

"Shut up. It's not like it's illegal to be in a 7-Eleven," Wil snapped, annoyed that April looked like she was going to cry. "Anyway, what are *you* doing here?"

"Same as you. I'm tired of all of that health crap," Colin explained. "I'm going to go look for some chips." The three made their way to the chip aisle while April continued to look around, as if she was afraid of being seen by more campers.

"So," Colin began, picking up a bag of pork rinds while he looked at her. Wil couldn't remember ever seeing eyes that were quite that blue before. "Wilhelmina, right?" He flipped the bag over and began to read the label on the back, leaning against the cheap aluminum shelving for support.

"Just Wil," she answered, fingering the Twix inside her shorts pocket. She picked up a package of Pringles next to Colin with her other hand and tried to decide if she should get them too. April followed, two steps behind her.

"Thought you were in, like, Wellness Canyon jail." He laughed. "I haven't seen you around much since the trust fall incident."

Wil smirked. She'd basically spend the first two weeks of camp hiding out in her room, hoping that skipping meals and activities would get her a few more demerits. "Nah, we're cool. Besides, that hike was the real torture anyway," Wil said confidently, looking him in the eye.

"Ha. True," he said. His blue eyes were filled with approval.

"Hi, Colin," April squeaked from behind Wil.

"Hey," Colin said, nodding in April's direction. "What's your name again? April?"

April grinned. "Yep. April Adams."

Wil nearly groaned at April's pathetic eagerness. She could just imagine April's pitiable attempts at school, sucking up to teachers and students. It would almost be funny if she weren't so earnest.

Colin picked up the pork rinds again, as if he couldn't decide about them. "I hate this walk-through-the-woods shit." He pointed at a lump in Wil's pocket. "What's that, a tumor?"

Wil reached into her pocket and pulled out the candy bars. "Just a joke—I'm going to buy them. My stash is running low."

"No kidding. I love Snickers," Colin admitted wistfully. "I used to have one before every practice. You know, just to keep me going. But Coach wants me to be faster. He said if I want to drop some poundage, I have to cut out sugar."

"Yeah, I've heard that one," Wil said, remembering when Ty had told her the same thing. She rolled her eyes in solidarity and led the way toward the front counter, squinting in the dim fluorescent lights.

Wil glanced around the glossy counter for any last-minute must-have snacks hidden among the trial sizes of Band-Aids, single packs of Advil, and displays of ChapStick. She grabbed the pork rinds out of Colin's hands and piled them on the counter with the rest of her booty and April's small package of Hershey Kisses, offering to pay for the whole lot. But when she reached into her pocket for her wallet, it wasn't there. "Darn," she said, patting her other pocket and turning back and forth from Colin to the greasy-haired teenager behind the cash register. "I forgot my wallet."

"No worries." Colin fished his wallet out from the pocket of his long shiny basketball shorts. "I got it."

Wil smiled as Colin stepped forward and paid the cashier with a crisp twenty and then folded the change into his wallet. The three filed out of the store and blinked when they stepped out into the bright afternoon sunlight in the parking lot.

"Are you heading back to camp?" Wil asked. She wasn't quite ready to go back to the confines of Wellness Canyon life just yet. Being in the 7-Eleven reminded her of all of the wonderful—and delicious—things she missed from the real world.

Colin shook his head and ran his fingers through his hair. "Nah, I know where we can wait for everyone to come back from their little nature walk. We can just sneak into the group," he said, motioning toward the woods that were in the opposite direction from where Wil and April had arrived. "That way we won't get busted."

Wil nodded, surprised by Colin's craftiness. Colin led the way toward the trees.

"Hey, check it out! Fat-camp runaways!"

Wil, Colin, and April turned their heads away from the woods and back toward the 7-Eleven, where two guys in crisp polo shirts—one with the collar turned up—were exiting a silver BMW.

"Moo!" The kids burst into laughter. Wil turned away from them, disgusted. Malibu was full of rich, entitled idiots like that wherever you turned, and normally it was just best to close your eyes and pretend they didn't really exist.

Colin, however, was clearly not of the same mind. "What'd you say?" he asked, stepping toward them.

"Are pork rinds on your *diet*?" one of the guys asked, looking a little afraid but not willing to back down in front of his friend.

"Oh, you're right, they're not. You want some?" Colin stepped forward and paused. Then he tossed the bag of pork rinds into the boy's face and punched the boy square in the jaw. The boy crumpled onto the pavement, holding his face. "What about you?" Colin asked the sidekick, cocking his fist again. The boy frantically shook his head and helped his friend up off the pavement. April and Wil gaped in awe.

"Hey, can you break it up?" The greasy eighteen-year-old cashier leaned out of the door, only half interested in the drama unfolding in the lot.

Colin reached down and picked up his yellow bag of pork rinds, opening the top and popping one into his mouth. "Want one?" he asked the blond kid, who was standing by the BMW, patting at his nose with a Kleenex. He turned back toward Wil and April. "C'mon. Let's get out of here."

The three of them headed back across the empty parking lot toward the opening in the brush, carrying their booty. "Nice punch," Wil said at last, once their sneakers were back onto the dirt ground of the woods. "That guy melted right into the sidewalk." Wil kept replaying the image of Colin swinging his fist into the other kid's smirking face. It looked even better in slow motion.

Colin smiled at her, flexing his hand and wrist a little.

"Oh, does your hand hurt?" April asked worriedly. She'd scooted over to the other side of Colin and was staring up at him with a blatantly worshipping glance.

"Nah, it's okay," Colin said, shaking out his hand. He stuffed one of the pork rinds into his mouth before folding up the bag and sticking it in the side of his shorts. Wil watched him lick his fingers.

"Dude, those things are like all salt," Wil commented. "*Yum,*" she added.

"They're gross, but good," Colin agreed. He held a branch out of the way as Wil and April passed under it, and suddenly, they were back on the well-worn dirt trail that they had deviated from only ten minutes ago. "I really wanted Cheetos, but they were all out."

"Oh my God, I *love* Cheetos!" April looked amazed, as if she and Colin had just discovered they shared a love for something completely unusual and profound.

"Oh my God," Wil mimicked, putting her hands to her face when April looked away. April caught her eye and glared.

"Hey," Colin said, pointing at the earbuds swinging out of Wil's shorts pockets. "What's on your iPod?"

"I'm sure nothing you'd know." She blew a messy curl out of her face.

"Yeah? Try me," Colin said, smiling.

"Regina Spektor, the Shins, the Thrills. I just downloaded the new Decemberists. I was supposed to go to their L.A. concert, but it's next week, so . . . yeah." She looked at Colin as if challenging him.

"That sucks. Have you heard of Someone Still Loves You Boris Yeltsin? Pretty sweet," Colin responded.

Wil almost stopped walking, she was so pleasantly stunned.

"Oh yeah. Where are they from again?" April asked, furrowing her brow.

"Please. As if you've ever heard of any of them before like five seconds ago," Wil told April. She looked surprisingly hurt.

Colin looked back and forth between the girls before answering. "Uh, I think they're from Chicago, maybe?" Colin scratched his chin, thinking. "Either that or San Francisco. I can't remember."

"I *love* San Francisco!" April exclaimed, instantly back to her peppy girl self. It suddenly struck Wil that every single sentence that came out of April's mouth had an exclamation point at the end of it. "It's *so* cool, there, you know? And people are super-friendly. I was in the Mission District this one time and—"

"Crap." Colin stopped abruptly, patting down his pockets. "I lost my room key."

"Are you sure?" April asked. She immediately whirled around on the trail and began retracing their footsteps.

"Yeah, I had it when I put my wallet back in my pocket at the 7-Eleven. It must've fallen out when I punched that guy."

"Do you want to go back?" April asked. "I can come with you." A gleam of hopefulness lit up her brown eyes. Subtlety, Wil noted, was not one of April's strong points.

"Nah," Colin said. "If you wait over there"—he pointed toward a fence of trees and scrub brush near a metal stake sticking out of the ground—"you'll hear everyone coming back and you can follow them back to camp. We really just took a short-cut." He winked at Wil, but she couldn't think of a response or a comeback before he turned back the other way and started jogging off.

"How will you get back?" April called after him, her voice tinged with worry.

Colin grinned. "I'll be fine. Later, ladies." Wil and April watched him fish the bag of pork rinds out of his pocket and shove a couple into his mouth before he disappeared through the trees. Jogging *and* stuffing his face? What an interesting specimen he was.

Wil and April trudged reluctantly toward their appointed hideout. The mood was deflated once it was just the two roommates again. Wil patted the pockets of her shorts, reassuring herself that the contraband was safe. Finally, April broke the silence. "Did you see how hard he hit that guy?"

"Yeah," Wil answered, a little curtly. If only her deadweight of a roommate would've buzzed off, she could've bonded with Colin over the Shins. They were silent for a few more moments, crouching in the brush until the sounds of power walkers drifted to their ears. Soon enough, the pack came into sight and once there was a break in the crowd, the two girls stepped cautiously out onto the trail, walking as if they had been part of the sweaty, out-of-breath crowd all along.

"*There* you are," a voice called out. Wil whirled around to see Paul huffing and quickly approaching them. So much for their brilliant plan to ease back into the group. Although his face was beet red and his shirt was drenched in sweat, he was still walking at a power pace, which impressed Wil. April and Wil waited for him to catch up, and when he did, Wil punched him on the arm.

"Looking good," she told him, not actually meaning it to sound as nasty as it did.

Paul didn't respond and instead started talking a mile a minute about all the species of cacti he'd spotted along the trail—apparently, he was something of an amateur botanist. Wil listened to him drone on, her legs aching as the woods finally opened up again and they appeared on the back side of the Wellness Canyon lawn. The group dissolved as the campers returned to their dorms for showers and some quiet time before dinner. All Wil could think about was sucking down her 7-Eleven booty—maybe *that* would curb her appetite enough to make the crap that was on the dinner menu palatable.

"I hope Colin gets back okay," April said as the girls closed the door to their room. "Hopefully the cashier didn't call the police. Do you think they'd arrest him?"

Wil regretted that there was no one there to appreciate her eye roll. Arrest him? Wil flopped onto her bed just as there was a knock on the door. April yanked it open and revealed an angry Melanie, her arms crossed over her chest.

"Hello, ladies," Melanie greeted them, her voice calm, almost friendly, even. "What happened to you two?" If Wil hadn't known better, she might have thought they were home free, but Melanie was examining each of their faces carefully, searching for the weaker link. At that moment, Wil almost respected her.

Almost. But not if she was going to take her Twix bars.

"What do you mean?" Wil asked, as innocently as possible. She pulled her T-shirt away from her chest and aired herself out, as if to prove to Melanie that she had, in fact, been power-walking all afternoon.

"On the hike," Melanie answered matter-of-factly, entering the room and shutting the door behind her. She stepped forward onto the hideous little pink rug in the shape of a heart that April had brought from home. "You know what I mean."

"We got lost," April blurted, wringing her plump hands. "We fell behind"—April's brown eyes glared at Wil to remind her whose fault *that* was—"and then we got lost."

"Hey, don't look at me." Wil innocently held up her hands and leaned back onto her full down pillows. She grabbed one from behind her and began tossing it into the air and catching it. Anything to get her mind off Melanie and April.

April started to whine. "I never said anyth—"

"Did you pick up some old friends on the way back?" Melanie interrupted, stepping forward. She grabbed Wil's pillow mid-toss and then pointed to the large lumps in her pockets. "Give them here."

Wil sucked in her cheeks, pissed off now. She slowly pulled out the candy stash, hoping the Twix was thin enough to remain undetected in her pocket.

Melanie turned to April. "Do you have candy too?" If anything, her voice was a little colder to April—as if she expected this from Wil, but not *her*. Wil smirked and quickly stuffed the Twix bar underneath her pillow while Melanie wasn't looking.

Melanie's full attention turned to April and she dug the bag of smashed, melted Hershey's Kisses out of her pocket. "Here," April said quietly, not making eye contact.

She put the little bag into Melanie's outstretched hands and Melanie softened her voice. "Eyes on the prize, April. Eyes on the prize. And for you, Miss Hopkins, this is two times in a week," Melanie reprimanded, shaking her head. "If I didn't know better, I might suspect that you were trying to get in trouble."

Well, of *course* she was trying to get in trouble—she wanted to get the hell out of here. But Wil managed to hang her chin in mock humility.

"So, who else was with you?"

The question startled April, and Melanie's hawk eyes flew to her. "Miss Adams?"

"No one," April squeaked, shaking her head a little too vehemently.

"Here at Wellness Canyon we have an honor code," Melanie said. "If you have something to say, now is the time to say it."

"And how does the honor code work again, exactly?" Wil said to Melanie.

Melanie smirked and tapped her clean white sneaker against the wooden floor of the porch. "You might find out firsthand," she said. Like *that* was a threat. Melanie gave Wil a penetrating stare before speaking again. "Get cleaned up for dinner. I expected better. From both of you." She closed the door behind her.

Wil watched through the window as Melanie hopped down the stairs and back to the Lodge. She stuffed the candy into the pocket of her knee-length khaki shorts as she cut through a makeshift game of Ultimate Frisbee on the lawn.

"I can't believe I got in trouble because of you," April said as she changed out of her sweaty T-shirt and grabbed her blue towel off of the corner of her wooden bedpost.

"Because of me?" Wil laughed, turning back from the view. "You were at the 7-Eleven too. Besides, if you hadn't been, you never could have flirted with *Colin*." Wil said his name in a mocking voice and then made loud slurpy, kissing noises.

April narrowed her eyes at Wil. "You are such a . . ." April started but didn't finish. She stood in her flip-flops, ready for a shower.

"What?" Wil countered, sitting down on her bed. "I'm a what?"

"Nothing. It's not worth it," April replied, storming around, grabbing her toiletries and slamming her dresser drawers.

Wil put her headphones on, letting the Yeah Yeah Yeahs drown out the noise. April slammed the door shut and Wil smiled slightly as she turned down her music. She sat up and looked out the window, just in time to see Colin bounding up the steps to his dorm, Rockefeller Hall, his pockets clearly stuffed with goodies. Suddenly, a summer at Wellness Canyon wasn't looking so bad after all.

# CHAPTER 11

**DATE:** July 8th

**FOOD:** 1 banana from the dining hall,
0 Hershey's Kisses

**EXERCISE:** Hike back from the 7-Eleven and
standing tummy tucks in the shower

AFTER HER SHOWER, APRIL TWISTED HER AUBURN HAIR INTO A ponytail and flipped it up, smoothing her hand over the back of her neck. She wondered if Colin liked girls in ponytails. She peered into the mirror above the teak dresser. April had noticed that Jessica's ponytail flounced from under her baseball hat in a hypnotizing fashion, swaying back and forth like a golden pendulum. April shook her head back and forth, trying to determine whether *her* ponytail could look like that from behind.

"What are you *doing*?" Wil's voice broke April's trance.

"Um . . . I was just . . . trying to cool off," April stammered. She plopped down on her bed and began sorting through the mail that she had picked up before her shower. Her limbs ached from the afternoon's excitement, as if she'd really gone on the hike with the rest of the campers.

"I can't get over the sound of that kid's jaw cracking when Colin laid into him," Wil said. She sat cross-legged on her unmade bed. "He really walloped that punk." Wil gave a quick one-two punch, her fists slashing the air, causing her Chocolate cell phone to crash to the floor. She didn't even bother to pick it up and make sure it wasn't broken.

"You should've seen him at orientation," April said, annoyed that Wil took such bad care of everything. If *she* had a cell phone, she certainly wouldn't throw it around.

"Yeah? I guess he's kinda cute in that totally typical not-interesting sort of way," Wil said, smirking.

April felt herself flush and quickly continued. "I mean, I spotted him right away. All the girls were swarming him." She paused, eyeing Wil. Was Wil interested in Colin, too? "He totally gave me a look." Well, maybe it wasn't *exactly* true that he had given her a look, but he had looked *at* her. Kind of.

Wil snorted. "Yeah?"

"Yeah." April twirled the ends of her ponytail around her finger and suddenly stopped and looked Wil in the eye. "I call dibs."

"Dibs?" Wil laughed. Sometimes April got the feeling that Wil repeated everything she said just so she could laugh at her even more. "You can't call dibs on someone. Especially someone that you have like zero chance with." She wriggled her sleeve and a Twix bar came sliding free. Wil unwrapped the candy loudly and took a chomp out of one of the bars without offering the other to April. *Where is her Twix etiquette?* April thought angrily. Everyone knew that if you opened a package of Twix in front of someone else, you had to offer them the other bar.

April flipped through one of the Danskin catalogs that Wil's parents had sent, not really looking at anything. "I have as good a chance as anyone else," she said firmly. She didn't really believe the words flowing from her mouth, but she knew she had a better chance than *Wil*, which was what she wished she'd said.

"Yeah?" Wil laughed as she loudly chewed her Twix. April recoiled in disgust at the chocolatey smell, reminding her of the one year she'd eaten all of the Halloween candy at once. "*I'm* more likely to hook up with him. And I have, like, zero interest."

"So you say," April answered, tauntingly. She had been so sick that Halloween that she'd had to stay home from school the next day, and the thought of malted milk balls still made her nauseous.

"What, you think I like *Colin*?" Wil demanded as she licked a chocolatey finger and then scooped an errant strand of gooey caramel into her mouth. She missed some, and the caramel dribbled down her chin onto a small silver heart necklace that April knew was from Tiffany. She had seen it in another one of Wil's catalogs. "Yeah, he's not my type."

"*Not your type?* It didn't look that way yesterday," April said, not backing down. If she let Wil push her around now, she was pretty sure that was what the entire summer would be like. "How about, first one to make Colin like her wins?"

Wil rolled her eyes. "C'mon, that's ridiculous! *Like her?*"

"Are you saying that you can't do it, then?" April stared at Wil.

"Of course I can do it. At least, I have more of a chance than you do, Miss 'Oh my God, I *love* San Francisco!' *Please,*" Wil said, laughing.

"Fine," April said, not dignifying Wil's joke with a response. "What are we betting on?"

Wil looked at April and grinned maliciously, crinkling the Twix wrapper in her hand and then tossing it into the trash can. "If I win, we go back to the 7-Eleven and you have to eat whatever I tell you."

"That's totally unfair. You know I'm actually trying to lose weight here!" April shouted.

"I know," Wil argued back, smirking.

"Fine," April huffed, thinking about the perfect punishment for Wil. Even if she had no confidence in her own abilities to snag Colin, she knew there was no way Colin and Wil would *ever* happen. She just had to think of something good.

"Can't think of anything? Want to forfeit?" Wil joked, scrolling through her playlist on her beloved iPod.

"No, shut up. Just let me think," April said. "If I win . . ."

Wil whistled the *Jeopardy* tune and it suddenly came to April. The perfect bet.

"If I win, I get your iPod. For the *whole* summer." April smiled smugly.

Wil looked shocked for a minute and April wasn't sure

what Wil would do. "Why didn't you bring your own iPod?" Wil finally asked, looking at April quizzically.

April felt her body flush with heat. She hadn't brought her iPod because she didn't have one. "I, um—I forgot it at the last minute. We were in a rush," she quickly covered her slip-up. Everyone at Wellness Canyon had an iPod—there were even docking stations in the computer labs. "But I totally miss it."

"Fine, whatever. Shake on it," Wil finally agreed, untangling her legs. She marched over to April's side of the room, holding her hand out in front of her.

"Okay." April firmly shook Wil's hand and then got up. "Oh, and by the way, don't forget to record that Twix in your notebook," she said sweetly. "You bite it, you write it." April smiled smugly as she left the room. She'd win that bet if it killed her.

# CHAPTER 12

**DATE:** July 9th

**FOOD:** ½ cup fresh fruit, 1 c. yogurt, 2 tbsp. wheat germ, vitamin C drop

**EXERCISE:** Early a.m. workout on the elliptical, level 8!

APRIL WENT TO HER EARLY MORNING WORKOUT ALONE THE NEXT morning because Wil had banged the snooze button three times on her tiny Tiffany & Co. alarm clock. It seemed supremely unfair to her that Wil should have such nice things and treat them so shabbily. Judging from her expensive-looking luggage, almost ruined by her stupid band stickers, she'd probably traveled the world—and complained the whole time. April had always wanted to go to Italy, but she'd heard way too many times that all the Italian women were incredibly skinny and beautiful and that everyone made fun of fat Americans. Besides, it wasn't like she and her mom could ever afford it anyway.

And of course, to top it all off, April couldn't believe that Wil was just wasting all of her time at Wellness Canyon while April was trying her hardest to make the most of it. She and her trainer were slowly building up weight resistance because April had expressed some interest in yoga. They were also getting her into some cardio. That morning, she had even done a whole forty-five minutes on the elliptical machine and she could already feel it.

April headed back to the room to shower before breakfast, but Wil still wasn't up. April showered and changed quietly and then went to the dining hall alone. She hoped to catch Colin and get a leg up somehow—maybe she could beat Wil to telling him how they'd covered for him with Melanie. That would score some points. But unfortunately, she managed to walk into the dining hall just as Paul and Dave did. All through the food lines, she couldn't get rid of them. By the time the three of them sat down at an empty table, Paul was already starting a story about a family trip to Paris. April scanned the room desperately for Colin but couldn't spot him.

"We visited the Eiffel Tower," Paul said, shoveling a forkful of egg-white omelet into his mouth. "The very top was closed, so everyone was on the lower deck and my brother and I were looking out at the Seine and this hot French chick tapped us on the shoulder and offered to take our picture. We gave her the camera and she took a picture and when she handed our camera back, we started making small talk with her, figuring she either didn't speak English or that she'd take off, you know? But she didn't."

"Was she a prostitute?" April asked jokingly. But then she wondered if her crude roommate was rubbing off on her. Dave and Paul laughed easily, though, so April ended up actually feeling kind of witty.

"No," Paul answered, waving one of his fat fingers at April. "It would be a much nicer story if she had been." He smiled wryly. "But so, anyway, she was real friendly and smiling and laughing with us and then she said, 'Have you ever heard of Herbalife?' She actually pulled a brochure out of her bag, with her card stapled to it, and handed it to us, like we weren't on vacation or anything. We pretended like we didn't understand her and walked away. She just shrugged and we watched her pull the same bit with another bunch of overweight Americans. Nice business, huh?"

"That's horrible," April said, shuddering. She caught Dave's eyes across the table.

"Totally messed up," Dave added, lifting a huge spoonful of cereal into his mouth. He frowned sympathetically at Paul as he munched, and it struck April for the first time that Dave seemed like a pretty nice guy.

Paul shrugged. "Yeah." He leaned forward to grab a napkin from the basket in the center of the table. "But that's when I decided to come here, so I guess it was sort of, like, I don't know. Fate."

She was in the midst of feeling sorry for Paul when she spotted Colin near the fresh fruit bar, mixing something into a green Nalgene bottle. He was wearing a pair of red Puma track pants and a white T-shirt and he looked like he'd just rolled out of bed. Her heartbeat quickened immediately, and her cheeks flushed. Seeing her chance, April stood up and grabbed her empty bowl, hoping that she looked casual enough, and headed toward Colin before he could be mobbed by his usual fan club.

"Oh, hey!" April said, scooping some yogurt into a bowl and browsing the fruit selection. She hoped he hadn't noticed her making a beeline for him.

"Oh, hey, April," Colin answered, yawning. His sun-streaked brown hair stuck up in a million directions, which April thought only made him cuter. Using a silver serving spoon, he took a scoop of bright red strawberries from their enormous silver dish and dumped them into one of the blenders at the end of the bar, along with the powdery contents of his bright green Nalgene. Colin turned his back to her and pressed a button. The blender whirled to life, instantly liquefying the concoction into a dark pink shake.

April waited patiently, adding a dusting of toasted wheat germ to her bowl until the blender stopped. "Oh, did you find your key?"

Colin shook his head. "Nah, I had to get another one." He poured the shake into his Nalgene and took a sip, grimacing. "Nasty." He grabbed the box of Splenda and pulled out a few packets, opened them, and dumped them into the shake.

April lowered her voice and leaned in closer to him, pretending to add some other goodies to her bowl. "Did you hear we got caught by Melanie?"

Colin set the box of Splenda back down on the bar and his dark blue eyes widened, so that April noticed for the first time that they were rimmed in brown. "You're kidding. What happened?"

Colin's sudden interest caused her hand to tremble and she set her bowl of yogurt down so she wouldn't drop it. "Well, she came to our room," April said, excitement creeping into her voice. "She totally pounced on us and confiscated all the candy."

"Wow. What did she say?" Colin asked. His protein shake sat on the counter, apparently forgotten.

"She wanted to know if we were with anyone," April replied coolly. "But we said it was just us." She shrugged as if it was no big deal, although she felt really pleased with herself to have not ratted out Colin. She gave him a quick smile and cocked her head, absentmindedly tucking some stray hairs behind her ear like Jessica. She wasn't actually sure if she'd ever flirted with someone before, but she hoped that she was doing okay.

"That was awesome of you." Colin grinned at her. The two of them stood quietly in the sunlight as several other campers moved around them getting their breakfasts. "So, uh, you were really going at it this morning," Colin remarked.

"What?" April looked at Colin questioningly.

"In the gym. You were really going strong on the elliptical. Do you do that every day?" Colin asked, still smiling at her.

"Oh . . . yeah. Thanks." April blushed and noticed that Paul and Dave were still watching her from their table in the corner. Then she refocused on Colin. She hated to think of him watching her work out—at least before she lost weight. "I like going so early. You know, get the pick of equipment." She could have kicked herself for making such lame conversation and tried to think of something witty to say.

But Colin grinned at her. "Well, you looked pretty awesome. Catch you later?" He winked before walking away with his protein shake.

April stood there dazed and grinning as Colin took off for the lawn. *Oh yeah*, she thought. Wil's iPod was as good as hers.

# CHAPTER 13

**DATE:** July 9th

**FOOD:** 2 whole-grain English muffins,
1 stack apple pancakes, 2 c. coffee
with extra soy creamer, 1 packet
sugar stolen from cute dishwasher
boy, and a partridge in a pear tree

**EXERCISE:** As if I'd give Melanie the satisfaction

WIL SAT ON HER BED AND TORE A PIECE FROM THE WHOLE-GRAIN English muffin she'd managed to stash in the pocket of her cargo shorts and popped it into her mouth. Last night, she had realized the folly of refusing to eat in the dining hall. If she was actually going to *gain* any weight—and thereby ruin her parents' dream of turning her into a Barbie doll—she'd have to load up on as many carbs as possible. In order to make it up, she'd scarfed a large helping of apple pancakes and stuffed two whole-grain English muffins into her pockets before leaving breakfast earlier this morning.

It was almost time for the morning activity now, and Wil was stalling until the last-possible minute. Just then, April

89

breezed into their room carrying a bright blue Wellness Canyon boutique shopping bag in her hand. She excitedly placed it on her bed and began rummaging around inside. April pulled a purple-and-turquoise Wellness Canyon–logo baseball cap out of the bag and cut off the tag.

"Oh my God, you have to be kidding me," Wil said, getting up to go look at the hat. "Did you actually pay money for that?"

"Yes," April replied calmly. "I think it's cute. Ooh . . . look what else I bought!" She reached down into the bag and pulled out a tiny purple calculator and proudly handed it to Wil.

"What is it?" Wil scoffed, not taking it.

"It's a calorie calculator. And it fits in your wallet!" April was clearly very pleased.

"Lemme see," Wil said, grabbing it now. " 'Nothing tastes as good as thin feels'?" she read off the top of the calculator. "You've got to be kidding me."

"Well, I think it'll be useful." April smoothed the top of her head and put the hat on, pulling her ponytail through the back.

"That ponytail makes your face look fat," Wil said matter-of-factly. She took a large bite of her English muffin and chewed loudly while April stared at her. "What? If your roommate doesn't tell you, who will?"

Fifteen minutes later, April was reaching back to help her up the red rocks, her face even more smiley than usual, which was extra weird, since Wil had lobbed a few more insults her way after the ponytail talk. "Thanks," Wil said, grunting and out of breath.

April dusted her hands off and flipped her ponytail. "You're welcome," she said. "You're supposed to use both hands, remember?"

*Yeah, yeah.* Wil remembered Melanie's hokey survival-and-navigation lecture before the start of the hike and how the rules of navigation would prove useful not just at Wellness Canyon but *in life.* She lived in Malibu, for chrissakes, not the Australian outback. Why would she ever need to know the best way to bend back brush or how to catapult herself up using small handholds on the sides of rocks? Who thought it was a good idea to have a bunch of fat kids do anything that involved catapulting? Wil wanted to know. Melanie's last piece of advice seemed particularly laughable: "If you get lost, remember to STOP," she'd said, drawing each letter with her finger as if she were talking to a group of deaf-mutes. "Stop, think, observe, and plan." On Melanie's instructions, they'd all faced north and stared at Huge Rock, the giant outcrop of red rocks that loomed over Wellness Canyon. "That's home base," Melanie said. "If you get lost, find your way to Huge Rock and we'll find you."

Wil struggled to the top of the embankment, a few steps behind April. She almost hoped she would fall backward off the cliff and split her head open. Or at least sprain her wrist. Maybe she'd get so hurt that Melanie would have to call up her parents and admit how second-rate this camp was in the first place.

And then they would whisk her home, and she could spend the rest of the summer holing up in her room with Netflix every day. *Ahhh . . .*

Wil surreptitiously chewed another hunk of muffin and slipped under a tree limb hanging over the trail. She going purposefully slow, but she was kind of curious about Melanie's tease about the "special event" awaiting them in the clearing at the end of the trail. Anyway, she'd be damned if she was going to let her curiosity turn her into a rabid camper.

"Will you please hurry up?" April pleaded, her face scrunched up in agony. "We're going to be last. Again."

"So?" Wil paused to pull up her socks, which kept sliding down her ankles and into her sneakers. "Who cares? You probably just want to catch up with your beloved Colin." She started walking again but even slower this time, just to frustrate April.

"No. I just want to know what the special event is. But maybe you're slowing us down to keep me away from Colin because you know that I have more of a chance than you," April replied, pushing her knockoff Chanel sunglasses back into place after they had slid, once more, down her sweaty nose.

"Oh, please," Wil said.

April stormed off ahead, and the space between the girls increased until April disappeared from Wil's sight.

Wil knew too well that if you falsely raised people's expectations, they'd expect more from you, like the time she'd gone all the way to the state spelling bee just because she could sound out words she didn't know. She didn't even want to take the flight to Sacramento—she hadn't known she was afraid to fly until that very moment—much less get up on a stage with a bunch of nerds and spell words that not even her parents knew the meaning of. In fact, her parents hadn't even made the trip, sending Wil with her fifth-grade English teacher as a chaperone, all expenses paid, her parents opting to attend an organic-herb-and-vitamin exposition in Santa Fe instead. Wil had convinced herself over the years that she'd lost in the first round out of spite, but in reality she'd had no idea how to spell *yawl*.

She heard a rustling in the bushes and wondered if there were rattlesnakes in the brush. Maybe one would bite her, and then she'd certainly have to be sent home. That is, if she didn't die.

Finally, following the fresh footprints in front of her, Wil showed up at the clearing, where the entire camp was waiting. Melanie and Kevin had been checking off the teams as they emerged from the path. Melanie smiled with relief at the sight of Wil. April stood next to them with her hands on her hips, scowling. "Well, someone has to come in last," Melanie said to Wil. "Twenty minutes, forty-three seconds. You should record that in your notebook so you know the time to beat next time."

Wil smirked and rolled her eyes, but Melanie and Kevin had already turned to face the other campers. "Time for our first competition of the summer—a scavenger hunt!" Melanie called out. "It's a Wellness Canyon tradition," she explained.

Her red hair was pulled off to the sides in little pink barrettes today, and Wil wished she could tell her that she looked like a crazy six-year-old. "Kevin is passing out the maps. Each person should get one." Kevin began distributing pieces of pink paper. "You'll see that it isn't *really* a map, but a list of geographical markers. These landmarks can be found down the dozen or so trails that spike off from the clearing."

Wil took a flyer from Kevin and scanned the paper, which was full of amateur scribblings of rocks and trees and a drawing of a river that looked like a long, wet tongue. Wil fought the urge to fold it into an airplane and send it sailing right into Melanie's hair. Were they *trying* to get people lost up here?

"The first to identify a landmark will find a colored plastic egg with a coupon inside. The coupons can be redeemed with me—and only me—for prizes generously provided by Wellness Canyon," Melanie said, referring to her clipboard. "This year the prizes are a yoga mat and DVD set, a Nike + iPod kit, a set of hand weights, a top-of-the-line pedometer, concert tickets, and a—"

"What concert?" Wil called out, interrupting Melanie.

Melanie searched around on a piece of paper, as if looking for details. "Um . . . something called 'Death Jam for . . .'" Melanie trailed off.

Wil laughed at her but perked up. "Death Cab for Cutie?" she asked, amazed at her luck.

Melanie still scrolled the paper before confirming. "Yep. Two of you will get tickets to their concert in L.A. next Saturday and will get to pick two friends to take off the campground for the night. Supervised, of course," she said, giving Wil a firm look. "And as I was saying, the last prize—the grand prize—is a one-year membership to Excalibur gyms!" Melanie looked right at Wil as the group erupted in applause. Wil flushed pink and then looked away.

"Okay," Melanie continued. "Here's how this will work. The prize eggs have two coupons for the same prize, one for each partner. You *must* search with your partner—look out for each other and work together. Anyone caught without his or her roommate will be disqualified and brought back to the clearing by one of the counselors. You'll work in pairs, but your total points will go toward your larger team. Each prize is worth different point values, which will be added up at the end, and each team will be ranked accordingly."

"Of course," Kevin added smiling slyly, "some of the plastic eggs are empty. If you get an empty egg, please collect it and give it to me or Melanie. Please do not re-hide the egg, or we'll be out here all day." A few people giggled, but Wil sighed heavily. She felt like she was at an elementary school birthday party run by a deranged mother.

"One very important detail," Melanie piped up. "Is everyone listening?" The campers quieted. "Do not cross any water," she said. "All eggs are on this side of any stream or river you run across. And remember: if you get lost, STOP," she said, drawing each letter with her finger. "Stop, think, observe, and plan." Melanie blew her whistle. "Go!" she shouted. The campers immediately scattered except for Colin, Gregg, Marci, and Jessica, who huddled in a group not far from April and Wil.

"Dude, I'm *all* over this one," Colin said loudly, bumping fists with Gregg.

"You wish," Marci said. "You couldn't find an egg if you'd laid it."

"Good one," Jessica said, high-fiving Marci, her blond ponytail bobbing perfectly.

Wil and April headed off in a direction opposite Colin's team—even though a huge group of campers had gathered around them and were following them down one of the trails. Melanie, Kevin, and the rest of the counselors fanned out across the clearing, some ducking down trails in advance of the scavenger hunters. Wil guessed they had to patrol the crowd so that a certain someone wouldn't be able to sneak off to the 7-Eleven again.

"Let's try over there." April pretended to look at her map and then pointed at the trail where Jessica and Marci had dipped out of sight. Apparently, Wil and April would be playing the part of paparazzi today.

"How sweet would it be to go to the Death Cab for Cutie concert?" Wil stepped carefully around a sharp rock that looked like it was begging someone to trip over it. She couldn't believe that she might actually get to hear some awesome music after all. It wasn't quite the Decemberists, but it was still good.

April nodded, giving Wil a sidelong glance over the top of

her sunglasses. "Or the gym membership. I've always wanted to belong to one."

"You don't already?" Wil asked, surprised. She thought that it was nearly a requirement of being fat and rich.

"Oh, well, I mean I always wanted to belong to Excalibur," April said, speeding up a little. Wil rolled her eyes, but followed her enthusiastic roommate.

Wil and April bounded down the trail in hot pursuit of treasure or possibly just April's new obsessions: Jessica and Marci. The trail forked immediately, and Wil could see over-sized bodies in T-shirts down both paths. "Let's take this one," Wil said, motioning toward the less-populated trail, squinting at her map. She paused and stomped her foot down on a root sticking up across the trail so that April didn't trip.

"Thanks," April said, her eyes wide.

"This way." Wil waved her arm, starting to get into it. She could picture the plastic egg—she imagined it was orange and yellow, jammed together to hold the tiny coupons revealing that they'd won the tickets. She wasn't thrilled that April would have to go with her, but maybe Colin could come too. Her pulse quickened.

Then she looked around and noticed that April had disappeared. Wil hiked back up the trail a few dozen yards, squinting through the brush. She finally spotted April's pale pink shirt down another trail. She was hovering about ten feet behind Jessica and Marci, who were poking a nearby bush with a stick.

"What are you doing?" Wil called out, irritated. She *was* like the paparazzi.

Embarrassed, April took a few steps toward Wil before tilting her head back toward Jessica. "I think this is the right way," she said, her voice hesitant.

"No! Let's keep going this way," Wil countered, waving her map around as if she could actually read it. "You're not going to find anything where everyone else is."

"Yes!" Jessica cried out in her tiny cheerleader voice, her high ponytail swaying. She snatched a green plastic egg out of the bushes and held it high above her head, as if there was a crowd watching her. She jumped up and down, sending up clouds of dust around her sneakers.

"What is it?" April asked excitedly. She rushed toward her.

Jessica cracked open the egg and two yellow slips fell out. Marci plucked them off the dusty ground and handed one to Jessica, letting her announce what the prize was. "Nike + iPod kit!" she squealed, her blond hair bouncing.

"That is *so* cool," April said, leaning in close to the girls and trying to get a peek at the little slip of paper.

"C'mon," Wil said, placing her hand on April's chubby forearm and yanking her away from the celebration. "If we want our own prize, we've got to keep our eyes open." She walked April back to their trail and continued ahead past a set of campers scrounging some underbrush off to the side. "We're looking for anything yellow, green, blue, purple, or pink—you know, cheesy Easter colors. Like your wardrobe." Wil smiled at April.

"There!" April pointed at the bottom of a scrubby-looking tree, ignoring Wil. Wil followed her finger to a yellow egg, looking like it was waiting for them.

"Sweet!" Wil quickly clambered down to the egg and picked it up, feeling her excitement swell. *Come on, Death Cab for Cutie!* She popped open the plastic egg. "Empty," she said, examining each half just to be sure.

"We'll find another one," April predicted, and for a few moments Wil really thought they might. The two of them feverishly scoured the rest of the trail, looking for anything that vaguely resembled the scribbled marks on the sheet of paper. Their trail finally converged with another one and spat them out right in front of Jessica and Marci, who had another egg in her hand.

"What was that one?" April asked excitedly, already heading over to them as if she had just been looking for the opportunity to ditch Wil. Wil glowered at her back.

"Empty." Marci wrinkled her nose and tossed the egg to April, who dropped it, then chased after it as it rapidly rolled toward a small ravine. Wil rolled her eyes at the fact that her roommate seemed ready to leap off a small cliff to snatch up anything that Marci or Jessica had touched.

Wil rolled her eyes. "C'mon," she called out to April. When her roommate didn't follow her, Wil looked back and saw that April had already managed to situate herself at Jessica's side, between her and the mass of other campers who had gathered to hear the magical story of how Jessica and Marci had found the iPod egg. "April!" Wil shouted, causing everyone to stop and look up like someone else had discovered another egg. April stared at Wil for a moment before shrugging and waving goodbye to Jessica, who didn't turn her blond head a single inch.

April jogged back to Wil, her long auburn ponytail swinging in a neat pendulum—she must have redone it for the millionth time today. "Sorry. We were talking about which trails had already been searched."

"Yeah, I'll bet," Wil fumed. She unfolded the list of landmarks and studied it again, her eyes burning. Even with her *real* Chanel sunglasses—a present from her mother, who said they'd make Wil look "elegant"—the glare of the sun hurt her eyes.

"That"—April pointed at an icon that looked kind of like a stalk of corn—"might be one of the markers," she suggested tentatively, pointing at a small clearing up ahead.

Wil looked to where April was pointing in the clearing and saw a slight bluish splotch in the otherwise green grass. "Oh my God! I see it!" Wil yelled, running forward. April followed close on her heels and the girls ran closer and closer to the plastic egg. But just as Wil got close to it, Colin and Gregg bolted out of the clearing and Colin ran straight at her, flirtatiously bumping her arm.

"Hey, watch it!" Wil said, but she laughed to let Colin know she was joking. She gave April a look that she hoped would encourage her to wait on the plastic egg. She didn't want to let Colin and Gregg know where it was if they didn't already.

"Find anything good?" Colin asked Wil, smiling. He wiped

the sweat off his forehead with the bottom of his cotton T-shirt. Wil couldn't help but take a peek at the hint of muscles visible on his stomach.

"I don't know, we're still looking," Wil said, looking at him and smirking. She couldn't believe she was being so flirtatious! "Why don't y—," she began.

"What's that?" Gregg suddenly screamed, lunging into the field. Then he jumped up and down with the small blue plastic egg in his hand. "Woo-hoo! We're going to Death Cab!"

"Ugh!" Wil crumpled up the map and threw it onto the trail. April blinked at the piece of trash before stooping down to pick it up and stuff it into her pocket. Colin winked at Wil and shrugged. For a second she thought he was going to ask her to join him. But then, to Wil's surprise, he winked and smiled at April too before running off down the path.

Wil turned to her roommate and glared. "If you weren't so busy drooling over Colin, we could have gotten the tickets!"

"Me!?" April screeched back, her hands on her hips. "You were the one who was talking to him." April glared at Wil before turning on her heels and walking away.

Wil kicked the ground in disgust and trudged back toward the center of camp. She couldn't believe she had been this close to going to see Death Cab for Cutie and it had just slipped through her fingers. But more annoyingly, she couldn't shake the fact that Colin had winked and smiled at April, too. It couldn't mean anything, could it?

# CHAPTER 14

**DATE:** July 15th

**FOOD:** 1 grape Vitamin Water, 1 whole-wheat English muffin with Tofutti cream cheese and then 1 whole-wheat English muffin <u>plain</u> after deciding that Tofutti cream cheese was gross

**EXERCISE:** That scavenger hunt was plenty to keep me going for a while.

SATURDAY AFTERNOON, WIL HEADED TO THE MAILROOM IN THE Lodge with a note that Melanie had slipped under her door, letting her know she had mail. She hurried down the hallway, excited by the off chance that one of her parents had taken pity on her and sent a care package full of chocolate chip cookies and the latest copy of *Spin*. Without saying anything, she handed the small orange slip of paper to the boy behind the counter. He disappeared for a moment, then handed Wil a large manila envelope with the Excalibur logo in the corner, the Wellness Canyon address written in her mom's neat cursive.

Wil tore open the envelope and unfolded the letter, shaking it for a hidden bill or two, but none dropped out. As she shook the paper, she realized that it was not in fact a letter, but an architect's blueprint with a huge pink Post-it note stuck in the corner.

> *Dear Wilhelmina,*
>
> *We had to redo the Palace (the water ruined the floor)—so we're redoing your room too. Thought you'd want to see the blueprint. You'll notice that we're putting in a huge walk-in closet for all your new (skinny!) clothes. Your father has authorized a major shopping spree upon your return to fill it up!! Stay strong—I'm sure you're looking and feeling better by the day!!*
>
> *Kisses,*
> *Mom*

Wil's throat started to burn as she struggled to keep herself from crying. She ripped the blueprint in half without even looking at it. Then she tore the halves into halves again. And again.

"Ooh, mail. Anything good?" Wil spun around to find Colin leaning in the doorway, the collar of his black Lacoste polo half turned up like he was some kind of hipster. Wil let the blueprint shreds flutter from her hands onto the floor.

"Nope." Wil tried to keep her voice light to disguise how much her mother's letter had upset her. "More like a 'Dear Wil, We-hope-you're-not-fat-anymore' letter from dear old Mom and Dad."

Colin snorted and stepped to the counter, leaning his elbow on it but still facing Wil. "I know exactly what you mean." He nodded at the kid behind the counter. "Anything for me?" The kid shook his head.

"Expecting a care package?" Wil had never realized how perfect Colin's skin was—like he didn't even have any pores. She resisted the temptation to reach out and put her hand on his cheek.

"Nah." Colin's normally light brown hair was wet and dark brown now, and he smelled faintly like Ivory soap. "I just told some of the college coaches they could reach me up here, so I thought . . ." His voice trailed off, his blue eyes clouding over a little. He glanced at Wil, like he didn't want to bore her. "My coach back home wanted me to go to sports camp, to work on my timing and skills, but my parents said no. They just think I need to lose weight. I dropped a few pounds here last summer and they were so impressed they sent me up here again. So . . ." He shrugged his muscular shoulders.

"Why didn't your parents let you go to sports camp?" Wil asked. "You would've lost weight there too." She regretted the comment as soon as it left her mouth. Even if they *were* at fat camp, it felt a little rude to point it out.

"Yeah, but they like the structure up here." Colin turned

toward the door of the office and paused to let her go through first, which struck Wil as surprisingly gentlemanly. "I got a list of exercises from my coach, though, so I'm keeping up. I usually work on drills out by Lake Jennings after lunch."

"My parents sent the blueprints for my new bedroom," Wil admitted, pointing at the pieces on the floor before they stepped out into the hallway. "They're adding a walk-in closet for all my new—and I quote—skinny clothes."

"Wow, that sucks," Colin said, his perfect eyebrows furrowing together over his even more perfect nose. Their sneakers stepped in sync across the wooden floor of the Lodge lobby. "Bummer."

"I think they're embarrassed of me because of their business," Wil said as the two of them stepped out into the bright sunny day. Some campers were out on the lawn, girls in tankinis lying out in the sun. She pulled her sunglasses down over her eyes.

"What do they do?" he asked, bending down to tie his shoe. He looked up at Wil.

"They, um . . . own Excalibur gyms," Wil said, searching the brilliant blue sky for a cloud. Each morning, she prayed for rain—she was getting a little anxious, spending so much time in the great outdoors. When was there going to be a good ol' rainy TV day?

"No shit! We've got one of those in San Jose." Colin stood up excitedly. He twirled a make-believe sword in the air and pointed it at Wil. "Come join the realm," he said, deepening his voice to mimic the idiotic television commercials her parents had paid about a million dollars for.

"That's it." Wil smiled. She could practically hear that voice in her sleep.

"Cool commercial," he added sarcastically.

Wil looked at him like he was crazy. "Whatever." She shrugged.

"Do you get to work out for free?" Colin asked, massaging the back of his neck. Wil tried to not watch him.

"Who cares?" Wil asked. The two of them just stood out in the middle of the front lawn. Other campers walked up and down the paths around them on their way to afternoon "share" sessions, as Melanie had named them. Basically, it meant sitting around in a circle and talking about feelings, which made Wil cringe just to think about it. She glanced at her Swiss Army watch with its green nylon band on her wrist.

"I asked for a membership for Christmas last year," Colin said, kicking at the lush green grass with one of his black Adidas sneakers. "But my parents didn't want me to. They said this"—he opened his arms, motioning to the Wellness Canyon grounds—"was my Christmas present. As if they're doing me a favor."

"Well, if it's any consolation . . ." Wil felt a smile tug at the corners of her lips. "I wouldn't work out at one of my parents' clubs if you *paid* me. They have this idea for a commercial starring them and me, but they're too embarrassed to put me in it. Which is how I ended up here." She worried that her rant was turning Colin off, so she lowered her voice an octave and uttered the other catchphrase the gyms were known for. "All for the glory of Excalibur."

Colin laughed and smiled at Wil, looking at her chest. "That's a great shirt," he said.

"Oh my God." She laughed, looking down at her VISUALIZE WHIRLED PEAS T-shirt. "You were totally just checking out my boobs."

"And what if I was?" Colin smirked.

"Well, it *is* harassment, sort of. But maybe you can make up for it by taking me to the Death Cab for Cutie concert with you tonight?" Wil smiled what she hoped was a flirtatious grin and leaned in closer to him.

Colin laughed and ran his fingers through his hair. "Oh, man, we already promised those to Jessie and Marci. But are you going to movie night tomorrow?"

"Dunno, maybe." Wil tried not to look as disappointed as she felt and put her hands in her pockets "Why?"

"Well, you should. I got to get going, but maybe I'll see you at the movie tomorrow?" Colin winked at her before he jogged down the pebbled trail, waving at a couple of kids playing soccer on the lawn.

Wil smiled as she watched him duck under a large tree and take a shortcut back to his dorm. Maybe she was missing Death Cab for Cutie, but this bet was going to be easy.

# CHAPTER 15

**DATE:** July 16th

**FOOD:** 1 small egg-white-and-fresh-herb omelet, ½ c. fruit, 1 c. mint tea with ½ tsp. honey

**EXERCISE:** 1 hour on the elliptical and 20 minutes on the bikes. But no Colin

SUNDAY AFTERNOON, APRIL HAD ANOTHER SUCCESSFUL WORKOUT session, and this time, she'd been careful to be sure that her hair looked cute—just in case Colin came in. She pressed herself harder than usual, getting in a full hour on the elliptical, followed by another twenty minutes on the bikes before she began her strength training. When her trainer came over to help her stretch out her tired muscles, he had told her that she was looking really great and April flushed from the compliment. She really had been working hard and she couldn't wait to see the results at the midsummer weigh-in.

After her workout, she showered and ate dinner with Dave and Paul and then went quickly back to Franklin before movie night. She'd been looking forward to the big outdoor movie night ever since it was posted on the bulletin board in the dining hall: she loved the movie *Overboard* and had seen it a thousand times. Goldie Hawn was so funny as a rich snob who got what she had coming to her, just like Wil would one day. At least that's what April hoped.

When April entered the room, she saw a note from Melanie tacked to the door, telling her that her mom had called. April's heart beat quickly in her chest. She missed her mom, and even though a lot of time had passed since she'd gotten the care package, April still didn't really have anything to say to her. She quickly tossed the note in the garbage can and then grabbed a sweatshirt and her pink-flowered comforter before heading back outside. April heard laughter and noisy chatter out on the lawn as soon as she stepped out of Franklin.

She noticed Colin, Gregg, and some of Colin's groupies spread out on scratchy wool blankets off to the side, under one of the leafy walnut trees on the lawn. Everyone faced in the direction of the enormous screen that had been wheeled onto the porch of the Lodge. April spread out her blanket on a patch of grass near Colin and the others just as the opening credits blasted through the space-age speakers.

April felt the cool summer breeze and she pulled her light sweater over her shoulders, loving how she could tell already that it was a little looser on her. Camp was hard—the hikes, the meetings, the talking, the lessons on nutrition and reasonable eating—but she was loving it. Or she would be loving it, if she had a decent roommate to share it all with.

With a sigh, she settled in for the movie. She glanced over at Colin as he tipped back his water bottle, taking a long sip. The crowd of campers laughed at sarcastic Goldie on the big screen and April laughed too, knowing the lines by heart. She felt guilty about how free she felt without Wil, but was that her fault?

Out of the corner of her eye, April saw Jessica and Marci join Colin and the others. Colin offered Jessica his water bottle and Jessica giggled, smoothing her hair behind her ear. She grabbed it and took a quick sip, making a face. A thrill of voyeuristic excitement ran through April as she figured out that it wasn't water after all, but vodka, gin, or some other clear alcohol. Jessica passed the bottle back to Colin and he took another big swig, letting out a long "ahhhhhhh" before wiping his mouth with the back of his hand.

April laughed loudly as Goldie threw Kurt Russell's toolbox into the ocean, hoping to draw attention to herself, but Colin and Jessica and the others weren't watching the movie at all. They were whispering loudly about something, and April couldn't hear. The night had become quite dark now and she could only make out the general shapes of the other campers. She settled back on her blanket and watched the movie, enjoying her temporary freedom.

A buttery, salty smell wafted across the lawn, tempting the campers from their blankets in twos and fours until the audience had been reduced by half. April thought about asking Colin and Jessica if they wanted anything, but she couldn't make out Colin's figure among those on his blanket, so she wandered the outer circle of the audience toward the delicious smell coming from inside the Lodge.

April's eyes adjusted to the sudden light and she followed the smell to its source, a full-sized air-pop popcorn machine someone had wheeled out near the bathrooms on the lower level. She watched as Paul filled two bags, leaving only a handful left under the yellow heat lamp. "The guy's coming back to make more," Paul said to her, though it sounded more like a question than a statement of fact.

Paul smiled at April, his lone dimple showing as he reached into one of his bags for a handful. He popped it in his mouth and then grimaced. "Ugh! What is this?" Paul said, running over to the garbage can by the stairs and spitting it out.

Just then Kevin wandered in. "Ah, I see you found our Camp Corn!"

"Camp Corn?" Paul asked, still trying to spit out the remnants of the gross snack into the garbage can.

"Yep," Kevin said with a smile. "No salt, no butter, low-calorie, non–genetically modified air-popped popcorn!" Kevin took a deep breath as he opened the door to the men's restroom nearby. "Enjoy!"

"Ugh," Paul looked down into his bag. "I don't think I can take two of these. Want one?" he asked, handing April a bag.

"Sure, thanks," she said, smiling up at him. He smiled back and then rushed back out to the movie. April looked down into the bag and grabbed a handful. She wondered how it could smell so good but taste so bad.

"Heeeeeey," a voice said near April, making her jump.

She whirled around and saw Colin laughing. April smiled, wondering what the joke was. As Colin drew near, she saw that his eyes were rimmed with red. "Gettin' some Camp Corn?" he asked.

April shrugged, looking at her bag. "I guess."

Colin steadied himself against the popcorn machine, and the old-fashioned wagon wheel rolled forward an inch or two. "Whoops," he said, removing his hand in an exaggerated motion.

"You like the movie?" April asked, smiling at him and helping to pull the popcorn wagon back toward them.

"Huh?" Colin stared at her.

She pointed vaguely in the direction of the lawn. "The movie," she repeated, hoping the popcorn guy would never return. "It's one of my favorites."

"Oh yeah," Colin said, rubbing his belly. He fished one of the kernels from April's bag and tossed it into his mouth. "Hey, you should come hang out sometime," he said, chomping the popcorn.

"I should?" April asked. Her face felt flush. "I mean, sure."

"It would be totally cool," he said, his eyelids looking heavy as he blinked. "Just really . . . fun." He picked out another piece of popcorn and munched it down; this time a small kernel stuck to his chin, right beneath his lips.

"Yeah . . . that would be great," April said, pointing at her own chin, trying to make him realize. But Colin didn't figure it out.

April opened her mouth to say something, but then she reached up instead, brushing the kernel from Colin's chin with her index finger.

"Hey, thanks." He stared at her and she felt her insides quiver.

She could feel Colin lean forward and when he did, the entire earth tilted, bringing his lips to hers. She could taste the popcorn on his acidic breath as his mouth opened against hers, but she didn't care. Her entire body vibrated as Colin pressed closer to her, cupping her chin as he kissed her and gently touched his tongue to hers.

She felt cold when Colin pulled away and smiled, taking her hand in his. "Anyway"—he lowered his dark blue eyes bashfully and gave her a crooked, intimate little smile—"so, um . . . I gotta get back." He jammed a thumb in the air and turned to go.

"Yeah." April smiled. "Okay." It took her a moment to realize that she'd won the bet hands down. April didn't even care about winning Wil's iPod—she just knew that it meant a lot to Wil, so she had to have it. No, April had won the grand prize. Not only had she kissed the cutest guy at camp, but he'd basically invited her to be part of his group. The thought gave her goose bumps and she rubbed her arms, grinning.

The door to the Lodge opened and Dave appeared with an empty popcorn bag.

"No more?" he asked, disappointed, as he stepped toward April. His cheeks were red from sunburn, and he was walking a little slowly, as if he was still feeling the effects of the afternoon jogging session.

"I think the guy is coming back to make more," April said, feeling a little deflated at talking to anyone else besides Colin. She glanced over Dave's shoulder as Colin disappeared into the woods behind the screen.

Dave's face lit up. "Righteous." He glanced around the empty lobby. "How many times have you seen this movie?"

"Oh yeah, um . . . a lot," April answered distractedly, heading for the door.

"See you later?" Dave asked, but April hardly heard him as she skipped out into the night, forgetting her blanket, a smile plastered on her face as she rushed toward Franklin, expecting to find Wil huddled in her bed with her iPod turned up loud. She couldn't wait to snatch the earbuds from Wil's diamond-studded ears and yell a loud "Ha!" right into them.

# CHAPTER 16

**DATE:** July 16th

**FOOD:** 2 helpings vegetarian goulash,
1 banana, 1 sugar-free Jell-o that
tasted like crap, and 1 Godiva
truffle from suitcase rations

**EXERCISE:** Well, if the walk back from the
Lodge counts . . .

WIL COULD JUST MAKE OUT APRIL'S LIGHT PINK SHIRT AND PERKY
ponytail as she wandered around the edges of the crowd, headed
back in the direction of Franklin. *That's odd,* she thought. Just
an hour ago, April was all about movie night. From her vantage
point behind one of the front pillars of Franklin House, Wil
could hear the muffled sounds of the movie and smell the faint
aroma of popcorn, though she had no interest in either. She
was still stuffed from the extra helping of vegetarian goulash at
dinner. She felt her bulging stomach to measure whether or not
her plan to gain weight was taking hold. If she could keep on
sneaking all the extra food, it just might.

She watched April disappear into the shadows of their

dorm, glad that she had vacated the premises for the night. She had wanted to stay in her room alone, but she had listened to every single song on her iPod about a hundred times and she was insanely bored. Wil rubbed her arms to ward off the evening chill and took a deep breath of the night air. She exhaled slowly but froze when she heard someone coming. The outdoor movie had been an optional event on the calendar, so she didn't think she could get busted for not being there, but she really wasn't in the mood to deal with Melanie tonight.

But it wasn't Melanie. Wil looked closer and peered through the bushes just in time to see Colin staggering a little as he disappeared down the well-trodden path leading up to Huge Rock. *He's drunk,* she thought, smiling to herself. She quickly looked around to see if anyone else was behind him, but he was alone, so Wil decided to follow—she didn't exactly have anything else to do. He weaved a little on his way up the quarter-mile trail and Wil kept a good distance between them, not yet sure if she wanted him to know if he was there.

When they got to the top, Colin just kind of stood there, fumbling with something in his hands. "Hey," she said, startling Colin. She wanted to speak first just in case Colin had been searching around for a place to pee or something. "How was the show?"

Colin stopped and looked around, confused, before his eyes focused on Wil. "Oh, hey. It was sweet. You totally shoulda been there." He swung an emerald green bottle of Tanqueray in her direction. "Want some?"

"No." Wil ignored the "shoulda been there" comment and wondered how much of it he had drunk—he looked plastered. "I'm allergic to whatever berry is in gin." She flashed back to the unfortunate discovery of *that* medical condition, the first time her parents left her alone for the weekend. She'd ended up in the emergency room with hives covering her entire body.

"There's berries in this?" Colin held up the bottle and peered into the green glass, looking a little disgusted. Wil didn't talk for a minute, watching him as he put the bottle to the side and began digging into the dirt with the toe of his shoe.

"You need a bigger shoe," Wil said, at last, figuring out that he was trying to bury the bottle. At the rate he was going, he'd still be digging next summer.

Colin poured the last of the alcohol into his mouth and then shook the bottle. "Huh?" he asked, turning toward her.

Wil could see his dark blue eyes glaze from the gin. "Here," she said, speaking slowly. "I'll help." She hopped down and dug her foot into the hole, loosening a wider circumference for the bottle. Neither of them spoke, but Wil could feel Colin's eyes fixed on her face, and she was grateful for the darkness so that he couldn't see her blush. When a big enough hole was formed, Colin laid the bottle in the tiny dirt grave and they both kicked the dirt until the bottle was concealed. "Perfect," Wil said, patting the dirt down with her hiking sneaker.

"What are you doing up here anyway?" he asked suddenly, leaning back against the rocks.

Wil laughed nervously and took a seat on a rock. "I was

just . . . hanging out." She was suddenly self-conscious about being off alone in the woods while everyone else was chilling with a movie. But whatever—Colin had left the party too, so she couldn't be the only antisocial person around, even if Colin had just come up to bury his liquor bottle.

"I love it up here." Colin leaned forward, bringing his face closer to hers. He slowly climbed up on the rocks and sat down next to her. He positively reeked of alcohol and Armani's Acqua di Gio, which Ty, her old trainer, always used to wear. It smelled better on Colin. "Very romantic."

A flutter of nervousness made Wil spring to her feet. "We should probably head back," she said, wondering what everyone would think if they saw her come out of the woods with Colin. "Don't want Melanie to catch us up here, right?"

Colin lay back on the rock and laced his fingers behind his head. "I gotta chill out." He stared up at the sky, where tiny flecks of stars were starting to appear. "Just for a minute."

Wil tried to relax and sat back down next to him, not too close but not too far away, either. She shivered a little in the cool night air and scrunched up her legs to her chest to try to stay warm.

"Remember what we were talking about before?" Colin opened one blue eye to see if Wil was still there, then closed it again, reassured. He went on without waiting for her to answer. "I didn't exactly tell you the truth about my parents. I mean, I didn't tell you the truth about why they sent me here."

Colin opened his eyes just as a faint cry of laughter went

up from the crowd, followed by a smattering of applause. He continued without waiting for Wil to respond. "My parents hate football," he said plainly.

"They probably just worry about you getting hurt, " Wil offered, noticing Colin's impossibly long eyelashes. She wanted to reach out and touch them with her fingertip.

"No, they don't care about *that*." Colin shook his head. "I mean, they care about that, sure. But they *hate* football. As in, they think all jocks and professional athletes are just dumb jerks who make a lot of money." He fumbled in his pocket for a second before pulling out his keys. On the key chain was a tiny round penlight, which he squeezed. The little light was remarkably powerful and lit up a fairly large circle at their feet. "They don't want me to go to USC."

Wil shifted against the rocks, aware of how uncomfortable they were. But it was nice to be alone with Colin, without his gaggle of groupies following his every step. "Where do they want you to go?"

"They both went to *Wesleyan*," Colin said, as if that explained everything. "That's where they met."

Wil had heard of Wesleyan before but didn't know exactly where it was. She didn't want to let on to Colin, though. "Are you going to apply?"

Colin laughed and ran a hand through his honey-colored hair, messing it up but in a way that managed to make him look extra cute. "My grades aren't good enough to even request an application." He gave a wry frown, and Wil was touched at the way he tried to disguise the bitterness in his voice by making a joke out of it. "They're probably not even good enough to get into USC, but who knows. Maybe I'll get a football scholarship. That's what I'm hoping, anyway. But I don't get why they have to look down their noses at sports, you know?"

Wil nodded and leaned back against the rock, looking up at the vast number of stars overhead. She couldn't remember ever seeing this many stars before, even in Malibu—the L.A. smog clouded the sky. "I know exactly what you mean."

Colin raised an eyebrow at her. "Yeah?"

"Well, I told you about my parents' commercial, right?"

Colin nodded.

"It's not just the commercial." Wil smoothed a curl behind her ear, not realizing until after she'd done it that it was something April always did. "My parents always say that having a chubby daughter is a public relations *nightmare* for their health clubs. Last year they won an award from the Greater Los Angeles Business Council that they were all excited about, but they wouldn't take me. They tried to play it off like they wanted to have this big romantic weekend at a hotel in downtown L.A. and that they were going to show their trust in me by leaving me home alone for the weekend, but really they were just too embarrassed to take me with them." Wil's voice broke and she coughed to cover, hoping Colin hadn't noticed.

"That's messed up," Colin said softly, sitting up and turning toward Wil again. She felt his hand reach out and touch her knee. Even through her jeans she could feel the heat from it. "That's really messed up. Only cowards are embarrassed by their family."

Wil felt a hot tear forming in the corner of her eye, but it dried up the second she noticed Colin lean in toward her. Almost hypnotically, she watched his blue eyes as they came closer and closer to her own until, at the last minute, they closed, and she felt his warm mouth kiss her. He opened his lips gently against hers, darting his warm tongue in just a little, then darting back out before grabbing for her bottom lip with his own wet lips. Wil kissed back, trying to follow his lead. He tasted like gin, popcorn, a trace of ChapStick, maybe.

Of all the times Wil dreamed about her first kiss—with some cute indie boy, at the back of a Sufjan Stevens concert in Santa Monica with her friends—she never dreamed it would be with a jock at fat camp. And she never, ever dreamed it would be this good.

A few minutes later, after she and Colin agreed they better head back before anyone got suspicious, Wil breezed past the remaining campers, who were straggling back to their dorms after the movie. If someone had stopped her and asked what she was smiling about, she probably would've confessed the whole stupid thing: that she'd made and *won* a bet about Colin with her lame roommate. And that to top it off, she *liked* him. And he liked her back. She wasn't too worried about April's feelings being hurt—it would be her own fault for not noticing that Wil and Colin shared a connection beyond "I like Cheetos too!" She could just picture the look on April's face when Wil forced her to eat half of 7-Eleven.

She burst into the room, half expecting to find April in bed, dreaming about Colin. But the room was empty, and Wil's heart sank. A few seconds later, Wil heard the sound of flip-flops thwacking against the hallway floor, and April bustled in through the door. Her thick body was wrapped in an unflattering pink bathrobe and her wet hair was twisted up in a towel.

"There you are!" Her face positively gleamed, and she bounced up and down on her flip-flops. "Guess what?" April laughed excitedly.

"Hold that thought." Wil threw herself down on her bed, unable to keep a grin off her own face. "I have something to tell you," Wil said in a singsong voice.

"No, shut up. This is really important," April continued excitedly, as if she couldn't care less what Wil said.

"*You* shut up. Let me talk!" Wil screeched. April's news could wait—she'd probably just discovered that both she and Jessica were Virgos or something. Besides, she loved the idea of teasing April first, making her beg for the information.

April finally backed down. "Fine. What?"

"If I give you three guesses, you'll *still* never get it," Wil said, folding her pillow and stuffing it under her head.

"God, Wil, don't play games. Just tell me!" April glared as she unwrapped the towel from her head and shook out her long mane of hair, sending a light mist across the room.

"Well, I don't know. Maybe you don't dese—," Wil started.

"I just kissed Colin!" April interrupted, apparently losing interest in whatever Wil had been about to say. April smiled her wide, goofy smile as she did a dorky little victory dance in the middle of the room.

*"What?"* Wil asked. Icy chills shot down her spine, sort of like an ice-cream brain freeze somehow extended to her entire body.

"At the movie," April explained, perching on the corner of Wil's bed. The top of her robe gaped wide to reveal her freckly chest. "We were just talking by the popcorn machine and he leaned over and kissed me."

Wil's mouth dropped open.

"What?" April quit bouncing and noticed Wil's reaction. "Is it *that* shocking that I could kiss him?"

"Um . . . only because *I* just kissed him," she spat out, furious at everyone—at Colin, at April, but mainly at herself for being so stupid. "Up at Huge Rock. We made out for like ten minutes," she added, even though that wasn't *exactly* true.

A dark cloud passed over April's cheery face and she looked like she might cry. "He kissed you too?" Her brown eyes went wide with confusion, and for a moment the two roommates just stared at each other. Wil could hear her pretentious little Tiffany clock, a going-away gift from her parents, ticking away, stupidly unaware of what was going on around it. Wil glanced again at April and felt a wave of pity for her. But just as Wil was about to say something, April spoke again. "So, well, I still won the stupid bet. I kissed him first. Besides, he asked me to hang out. So clearly, I won."

123

"The bet was who could get Colin to like her first," Wil pointed out, quickly stomping out any feelings of pity for April. "And since I just kissed him, he *obviously* doesn't like you."

"That doesn't make any sense," April whined, scrunching up her face in disapproval. She slowly stood up from Wil's bed and walked over to her dresser.

"You lost fair and square," Wil said, feeling even nastier now. She pulled back the covers to her bed and stared at her dark red Ralph Lauren sheets. She wished she could crawl into them and never crawl out again, or at least, not until the end of the summer. "Plus, he was probably *drunk* when he kissed you. You shouldn't let boys kiss you when they're drunk." Wil left out the unfortunate truth: that he had been drunk when he kissed her too.

"Um . . . now you sound like the drunk one." April picked up her plastic hairbrush, looking like she wanted to throw it at Wil. "He kissed me in public. During the movie."

"Well? It couldn't have been that good if he came after me!" Wil countered.

"Yeah, but Colin didn't ask you to join his group, did he? I mean, he practically asked me to be his girlfriend," April asked defiantly, brushing through her wet hair. "He *specifically* asked me to hang out with him, Gregg, Jessica, and Marci sometime."

"*Specifically* asked you *sometime*?" Wil repeated. With her back to April, she quickly stepped out of her jeans and pulled on the Calvin Klein men's boxers she slept in, the elastic waist tight against her skin. "That was very kind of him. I'm totally sure he meant it."

"Just wait until breakfast," April snapped angrily, waving her brush around in the air. "You'll see what I'm talking about. And you're gonna feel like the *jerk* that you are. Like everyone *knows* you are. Oh, and by the way, you better listen to your iPod all night because it's going to be a long time before you have any music again."

"Kiss my ass," Wil said easily. "Get ready to eat your weight in Snickers tomorrow." Wil and April just stood and stared at each other defiantly until April finally stormed out of the room to brush her teeth.

Wil pushed away her feelings of disappointment over Colin away and climbed into bed with a smug little grin on her face, imagining how miserable she would make April tomorrow. And it felt great.

# CHAPTER 17

**DATE:** July 17th
**FOOD:** 1 large carrot-bran muffin ... and my entire stash of Godiva
**EXERCISE:** Eating my entire stash of Godiva

THE NEXT MORNING, WHILE APRIL WAS FINISHING UP HER WORKOUT, Wil headed over to Dickinson, where she spotted Colin as soon as she entered. As usual, he was maneuvering his way around the fruit bar, preparing his protein shake. She hadn't even bothered to shower, throwing a gigantic hoodie on over her black Hanes T-shirt. She spotted April come in and linger in Colin's general vicinity, probably trying to manufacture a bump-into or some other idiotic move.

Wil, however, didn't need to manufacture anything. She brushed directly past Paul and Dave in the corner, calling out to her. She marched up to Colin and loudly cleared her throat.

"Oh, hey." Colin yawned, a little groggy. His eyes were red and he kept squinting at the sunlight streaming in through the windows. In addition to his green Nalgene bottle, he was also holding an empty Wellness Canyon–logo plate in his hands.

"Hi," Wil said, angrily tapping her sneaker against the green tile floor. "Anything you want to tell me?" Wil was a little surprised at how much she sounded like her mother.

"Huh?" Colin scratched his matted hair and Wil noticed that he too hadn't showered. "What do you mean?"

"What do I mean?" Wil repeated. She was too irate to pick up one of the steaming-hot plates, fresh out of the dishwasher.

"Yeah," Colin said, starting to look annoyed. His blue eyes were cold and when his lips weren't curling into a crooked grin, he was nowhere near as attractive. "What's going on with you?"

"What did you mean by kissing me last night?" she spit out angrily, unable to complete the sentence: *if you'd already kissed April?*

"Whoa," Colin said, lowering his voice. "Let's keep that quiet." He laughed uncomfortably, his squinty eyes darting around the room. "We were a little wasted."

"I wasn't wasted," Wil said matter-of-factly.

His eyes met hers and for a moment she saw some of the softness that had been there last night. "Oh. Maybe it was just me," Colin admitted.

The line moved and Colin and Wil shuffle-stepped forward.

"It was just you," Wil confirmed loudly, boring through his head with her glare.

"Hey, shhh . . . ," Colin said sternly. A flash of anger passed across his normally cool-as-can-be face. "Geez, I can see why your parents are so embarrassed of you now."

Two girls sitting at a table nearest the breakfast bar snickered at Wil and tried to hide behind the broccoli-shaped tea cozy on their table. Wil turned and stormed off, almost flipping a tray full of food out of the Paul's hands as he headed to his table. "You okay?" Paul called, steadying his tray, but she was too furious to stop and tell him she was fine or even apologize.

Instead, she stalked over to the fruit bar, where April was filling a white ceramic bowl with freshly sliced kiwi and yogurt. "You can have him," Wil spat out, her voice shaking. She shoved her earbuds into her ears and blasted her music as she stomped toward the door, stopping only to snatch a carrot-bran muffin on her way out.

# CHAPTER 18

**DATE:** July 17th
**FOOD:** Too nervous to eat . . .
**EXERCISE:** 60 minutes on the elliptical!

APRIL COULD BARELY KEEP HER TRAY FROM SHAKING AS SHE MOVED through the breakfast line. She placed a plate with a small fresh-herb-and-egg-white omelet next to her bowl of kiwi and yogurt sprinkled with wheat germ, keeping one eye on Colin the entire time. Wil had made a fool out of herself—and if she ever had a chance with Colin, it was certainly gone now. April had hardly been able to sleep the night before, the image of Wil and Colin kissing up at Huge Rock was so burned in her brain. She had thought about it all night, trying to figure out why Colin would have kissed both of them. But then she had almost laughed when she remembered the alcohol. Colin had been a little tipsy when he kissed her, and April realized excitedly that he must have been totally trashed by the time he kissed Wil. He probably thought he was still kissing April! Now she felt a little sorry for her roommate—just being the recipient of someone's drunken kiss. Then again, Wil had kind of asked for it. That was karma for you.

Paul and Dave waved to April as she left the breakfast bar, motioning toward an empty chair at their table, but April pretended not to see them. Instead, she sauntered casually toward Jessica and Marci, who were pulling apart their breakfast burritos, Marci piling the fake meat off to one side of her plate. April stood at the table and smiled, hoping for Jessica to ask her to sit down in one of the many empty seats at their table. But Jessica just looked up and smiled while Marci stared on, meticulously chewing a wad of egg and fat-free cheese. A look of confusion soon replaced Jessica's smile as April set her tray down across from them and pulled out a seat. April felt her heart beat faster as she tried to think of something to say.

She was saved, though, by Colin—ever the white knight in mesh lacrosse shorts—when he put his tray down next to hers and sat down. "Hey," Colin said.

"Good morning," April said. She imagined it was the same tone she would have used if Colin were her husband and they'd just woken up and eaten a delightful breakfast together after going on a four-mile jog along the beach in coordinated workout clothing.

Colin glanced at Jessica and Marci, who both smiled back at him, although their smiles looked kind of strained. April figured that they must not have been expecting Colin to bring her to their table already. April wondered for an exhilarating moment if he was going to introduce her as his *new girlfriend* or if it was too soon for that.

"You should really try the egg-white-and-fresh-herb omelet,"

April said enthusiastically to no one in particular. "It's delicious." Marci stared at April's omelet and April realized that she actually had yet to take a bite.

Colin turned to her. "So . . . um," he started, as Gregg joined them at the table.

"Yes?" April asked. *Yes, dear?*

"You're . . . sort of sitting in someone's chair," he said, his hand resting on his fork as he looked pointedly at the white wicker chair April was seated in.

April searched his face for the hidden joke she was sure they were sharing but couldn't figure it out.

"What I'm saying," he said, after she kept staring at him blankly, "is that you're . . . sitting . . . in . . . someone's . . . chair."

Marci hid a smile and Colin laughed. April felt her cheeks burn. She knew someone like Wil would have been able to come up with some sort of devastating comeback that would turn the whole thing on Colin and make him feel like the idiot, but her brain didn't work like that.

April calmly picked up her tray and stood up, leaving the table quietly and quickly as Gregg snickered. April vowed to herself that she would make it out of the dining hall before anyone saw her cry.

# CHAPTER 19

**DATE:** July 17th
**FOOD:** ½ carrot-bran muffin. And I only
ate that out of spite.
**EXERCISE:** Does telling off Colin count?

WIL KICKED THROUGH THE PILE OF DIRTY LAUNDRY AT THE FOOT OF
her bed, scattering her clothes. The image of Colin's smirk,
his words, *I can see now why your parents are so embarrassed
of you,* replaying so loudly in her head that not even the new
L7 album on her iPod could drown them out. She had nobody
to talk to about how horrible she felt, and soon, she wouldn't
even have her music. Wil turned up the volume and collapsed
onto the bed.

Her body trembled as she recalled all the personal things
she'd confessed to him, both in the post office and up on Huge
Rock. One second she felt like she might throw up, the next she
wanted to put her fist through the wall.

The door swung open and April appeared, a scowl across
her dopey face. Wil grabbed her key, ready to run out of the

room, but stopped when she noticed April's lips quivering. "What's your problem?" she asked. Maybe she wasn't about to lose her iPod after all. . . .

"Nothing," April said as the first tear slid down her nose and hung on her lip. She wiped at it with the back of her hand and looked away. "What do you care?"

"What? Colin doesn't like you, either?" Wil remarked, picking up her towel and shower caddy.

"No, okay? Are you happy now that I'm miserable too?" April said, taking a paper napkin from her pocket and blowing her nose.

"Well, if you're crying over Colin, you should just save it," Wil advised. She would have thought she'd be happy to hear that Colin had rejected April, too, but she just felt sorry for her. April wasn't as tough as Wil was, as evidenced by the way she was just about hyperventilating. "He's not worth it."

April shook her head. "Just drop it, okay? I don't want to talk about it." She disappeared for a moment, down the hall, then reappeared carrying a gold box of Kleenex from the bathroom. She blew her nose, loudly.

"*Drop it?*" Wil asked incredulously. "Are you crazy?" Did April have no self-respect? She was just going to roll over and forget about Colin humiliating her in front of her idol, Jessica? Wil got up and grabbed her towel on her way out the door. "Well, you can do whatever you want, but I'm not about to just let him get away with it." She slammed the door behind her and stormed to the shower to plot her revenge.

# CHAPTER 20

**DATE:** July 22nd
**FOOD:** ¾ cup Kashi cereal, ½ c. skim milk, and 1 handful fresh strawberries
**EXERCISE:** I've heard that crying burns a lot of calories. Well, if that's true, then I'm home free.

APRIL STOOD OUTSIDE THE DOOR AS THE LAST MEMBERS OF A yoga class trickled out, waiting to do her own exercises in the workout room. When the room had emptied, April went in and stared at her body in the long wall of mirrors. She silently did some calf raises, stretching out her hamstrings as the trainers had taught them to do before exercising. She flexed her bicep in the mirror, admiring the slight shadow that was starting to form under her muscle. She'd always known it was in there somewhere.

"Hey!" April dropped her arm and turned to see Dave standing in the doorway. He was dressed in his workout clothes—a pair of black Adidas track pants and a black T-shirt that hung a little loosely on his shoulders. "Getting in an extra workout?"

April considered lying, pretending like she'd just finished, but before she could answer, Dave added, "Me too."

"Oh, cool," April said, hoping he hadn't seen her admiring her own bicep. She grabbed one of the thick blue exercise mats that reminded her of the ones they used in gym class at home. Dave followed her to the stack by the door and grabbed one of his own. Both of them plopped their mats down on the smooth, polished hardwood floor, near the ballet bar bolted to the mirror.

"Do you mind if I work out with you?" Dave asked before getting down on his mat.

April shrugged and shook her head, feeling the tip of her ponytail tickle the back of her neck. "No."

"So . . . uh . . . what are you going to do?" he asked as he awkwardly lowered his body onto the mat.

"Just some stretches and squats," she answered. "Maybe some crunches. Oh, and leg raises."

"Mmm . . . gotta love crunches," Dave joked, stretching out on his mat. "I just can't get enough!" He patted his abs and grunted as he did a sit-up, raising his elbows to his knees.

April laughed and for a moment they both lay on their mats and stared at the high ceiling. Then they got down to work, stretching out. April bent her right leg and pulled it across her body as far as she could, alternating with her left. Her muscles were still sore from the morning workout and she liked the idea of pushing them further. The burn actually felt pretty good in a weird way.

"So what's the deal with Wil?" Dave asked. He tucked his knees as close to his chin as possible and held the stretch.

"Yeah, I know," April said. "She can be rough."

"No kidding. I don't know how you live with that," Dave said, exhaling loudly. His crew cut was growing out a little, making him look cuter than April had thought he was at first.

"So," he began, and he grew a little quieter. "This guy Jeff—do you know him? Anyway . . . he's in my share group and he told me that Wil and Colin, like, hooked up. Is it true?"

"Gross," April said, wrinkling her face in distaste. April hated to think that they'd both ever actually liked Colin and she *certainly* didn't want other people talking about it. April was surprised at how defensive she felt about Wil, even though she'd spent most of the summer hating her. "I doubt it. He doesn't really seem her type." She lifted her right leg a few inches off the ground and held it, keeping her hands by her side and pulling the muscles in her stomach tight.

"Speak of the devil," Dave murmured under his breath as Colin walked in, studded with ankle and wrist weights. Dave and April exchanged a glance and April had to fight to stifle a giggle. Colin barely acknowledged them and instead turned and admired himself in the full-length mirror next to the door, clearly proud that he had an audience.

April knew she should ignore him, even though she really wanted to go over and punch him right in the face. She rolled her eyes. "So, what's your school like in Phoenix?"

"Eh, I don't know. Bunch of rich jerks." Dave shrugged, lifting his chest up toward his knees. "I go to this all-guys Catholic school. It's really good, but I hate it." Dave breathed heavily as he rested his head on the mat for a few seconds. "It's really competitive, like everyone's trying to get into Harvard or something. But really, they all go to Notre Dame and get in because they're good at sports or have a lot of money or whatever." Dave glanced over at Colin, making sure he wasn't paying attention. "So it doesn't matter what kind of grades you get anyway."

April rolled her eyes and lowered her voice. "*That* sounds familiar."

A loud screeching noise filled the workout room as Colin started sprinting back and forth across the polished hardwood floors, his sneakers squealing to a stop just short of the wall each time before he lunged back in the opposite direction.

"I need some water." Dave lumbered to his feet.

"Watch out." April smiled, nodding in Colin's direction. Dave saluted and darted through Colin's erratic workout toward the water fountain just outside the gym door. April stood up and bent her knees, concentrating on keeping the correct form that Cammie, who did the morning aerobics classes, had shown them. As she tightened her stomach muscles and kept her back straight, she felt a weird, sliding sensation. It took her a second to realize what it was, and she instinctively grabbed at her shorts just as they slipped off her waist.

"Hey, Grandma. Nice underwear." April heard slow applause and she whirled around to see Colin staring at her with a huge grin on his face. "But you should know I don't really want to see you without your clothes on." He smirked, puffing out his chest.

April felt her face turn bright red. *Of course* she hadn't had a chance to do laundry and was, therefore, wearing her ugliest, oldest, and largest pair of underwear.

She grabbed her mat and charged past him, almost running smack into Dave as he returned from the water fountain, wiping the water from his face.

"You all done?" Dave asked, looking confused, but April could only manage a brief smile as she dropped her mat messily on top of the stack and marched out of the gym. Suddenly she wasn't so sure she wanted Colin to get away with it either. And she knew just the girl to talk to.

April stormed back across the lawn and down the pebbled path to Franklin, scheming the whole way. She jogged up the porch steps and into their room to find Wil stretched out across her bed, listening to her iPod, as usual. April went over to the bed and motioned for Wil to take out her earbuds.

"You know that revenge you were talking about?" April said loudly, wiping the sweat from her forehead. Wil nodded slightly, her eyes open wide as she looked back at April. "Well," April continued. "I'm in. Totally."

Wil's face broke into a broad smile. April grinned back.

# CHAPTER 21

**DATE:** July 25th

**FOOD:** 1 ripe apple with 2 tsp. peanut butter and wheat germ

**EXERCISE:** 45 minutes on the elliptical and 10 reps of bicep curls. I think I'm starting to see a difference!

"GOT IT!" WIL SNAPPED HER CHUBBY FINGERS AS THE TWO OF them climbed the steps to the Lodge a few days later for their scheduled midsummer weigh-in. April whipped her head around and grinned.

"What is it?" April asked. Wil started to climb faster as she turned her idea—whatever it was—over in her head, and April had a hard time keeping up. They joined the stream of other campers making their way into the Lodge, all carrying their little green weigh-in reminder slips.

"Tell you later," Wil said under her breath as they approached the line.

April felt like all of her energy over the past few days had been spent on working out, avoiding Colin's group at all costs, and scheming ways to get back at him. The only time she and Wil actually seemed to get along was when they were planning their revenge. Even then, though, Wil seemed to shoot down all of April's ideas—so far they'd thrown out putting red ants in his bed, smearing peanut butter inside his sneakers, and stealing everything from his dorm room and dumping it in Lake Jennings. April still felt humiliated enough to keep after it, searching for the perfect revenge.

April had no idea what to expect from the midsummer weigh-in. In fact, she'd almost forgotten about it until right before lunch, when she and Wil saw the line of campers waiting in the Lodge lobby, Melanie perched next to the scale. They had rushed back to their room to grab their notebooks and then hurried back to get in line.

Up ahead, April could see Jessica and Marci waiting their turn. Neither looked like they'd lost any weight, but it was hard for April to tell—they didn't have too much to lose to begin with. She'd stayed away from Jessica and the others since her dining hall fiasco, avoiding Colin's group entirely if she could help it.

Jessica looked back abruptly and April averted her eyes, shading them as if she were searching for someone—Dave and Paul maybe, since, besides Wil, they were really the only people who talked to her.

The scales in the Lodge were tucked into an alcove behind a half wall that swung out like a fence gate. She and Wil stepped toward the scales and Melanie hovered next to them with her

BlackBerry in one hand, the other moving the sliding weights until they balanced. April remembered the first weigh-in with Dr. Hausler. The scale seemed friendlier now that the little screen read a number well below 200. "You've lost twenty-two pounds," Melanie noted, entering the information into her BlackBerry. "Great work, April!"

April wanted to pump her fists in the air. The Wellness Canyon brochure said campers could lose up to five pounds a week and she'd lost almost five and a *half* pounds a week. Even though April had known she was losing weight, it felt different when she knew how much. *Twenty-two pounds,* she thought in awe, feeling almost ready to cry. She couldn't wait to tell her mom.

"Gain of three," Melanie said, not very quietly, looking at Wil's scale. "Step down and step up again," she directed. Wil did as Melanie asked. "Same." Melanie's voice was clipped, and she was clearly not happy.

"Funny, I thought it would've been five," Wil answered sarcastically, hopping off the scale. "I'll try harder next time." She patted her fat stomach. "Might have to cut out vegetables altogether." April watched as some of the other girls behind them giggled.

Melanie put her BlackBerry down and pulled Wil and April aside, out in the hallway. "You guys *have* to look out for each other," she scolded them. Wil wriggled free of Melanie's grasp as April looked on. April considered tattling on Wil, about how Wil ate everything she could stuff into her mouth during meals and how she filled her pockets for later, too. What was April supposed to do, risk injury to life and limb and reach into Wil's garbage disposal of a mouth and rip out the food? "I told you that roommates here are important," Melanie prattled on.

"So important," Wil interjected sarcastically, twirling the ends of her hair around her finger.

Melanie's eyes bored through Wil as she continued. "I have seen too many people go through this camp and I know better. You can't do it alone. I couldn't do it alone. I had a wonderful roommate and it's about time that *you* learned to work together. Think about it," Melanie finished, and went back into the little alcove to finish weighing the rest of the girls.

April scowled and looked like she was about to cry, but Wil just looked smug. "What? You don't buy her crap, do you?" Wil asked her roommate.

"You are *unbelievable*," April muttered angrily as she stormed down the hallway and out the Lodge door. She looked out over the lawn and Lake Jennings. The whole camp seemed cheerful, full of laughter and sunlight. It contrasted sharply with her horrible mood. April thought about her roommate and sighed. So much for actually relying on each other.

# CHAPTER 22

**DATE:** July 25th
**FOOD:** 1 c. brown rice with steamed broccoli and soy sauce. And 1 macrobiotic cookie—surprisingly yummy
**EXERCISE:** Power-walked 3 times around the lawn after lunch

THE COMPUTER LAB WAS EMPTY SAVE FOR A LONE COUNSELOR checking his e-mail. He didn't look up as April entered and found Wil at a cubicle at the opposite end of the lab. She'd managed to all but ignore Wil in the lunch line, turning her attention instead to Dave and Paul, who were grumpy about not having lost more weight—even though April had tried to assure them that they had probably just gained some muscle.

Wil didn't look up as April approached her, the light from the monitor reflecting in her blue eyes. "What are you doing?" April asked, annoyed that Wil had insisted they meet here after this morning's weigh-in disaster. April looked around at all the shiny white iMacs. She'd never had a reason to come here before—her mom didn't have a computer, so it wasn't like she ever got any e-mail.

"There's this really cool website that will send you books and shampoo bottles and stuff filled with candy," Wil whispered, in case the counselor was listening. She didn't remove her eyes from the screen. "It's for, like, prisoners or something. Look at this one." She pointed at a flowerpot. "The entire thing is edible. It's made of sugar. Even the dirt."

"Grow up," April said, crossing her arms over her chest. "Is this what you wanted to show me?"

Wil rolled her eyes. She clicked the mouse and the page disappeared, revealing the desktop with the Wellness Canyon logo. "Actually, no," she said, glancing across the room at the counselor, who pushed back his chair and stood up. He stretched his arms over his head, revealing his almost six-pack abs before nodding in Wil and April's direction and disappearing out the door.

"Okay, so you know how Colin is always bragging about how good he is at sports?" Wil asked, looking up at April excitedly.

April nodded bitterly. "The other day he ran into Dave while he was chasing down a Frisbee. He knocked him over." She thought of Dave on his back, his legs kicking in the air like a helpless bug that couldn't turn over. Colin didn't even give him a hand getting up.

"Right." Wil grinned wickedly, though April had no clue what she was getting at. "He does extra workouts on his own, did you know that? He's got like a list of stupid things he does to keep in shape for football. Lame, right?"

April thought that it was actually a pretty good idea, which made her even madder. If exercising was so easy for Colin, why was he even *at* Wellness Canyon? Everyone else struggled just to keep up and he was doubling his workouts in private.

"He checks the post office for a letter from USC like every hour," Wil went on. She clicked the mouse and the University of Southern California home page came up. "So I thought we would give him what he's been waiting for." Wil's eyes sparkled with a glee April hadn't seen before. She was positively *glowing*. "I mean, it's very sad that they've rejected him, but at least he won't have to run to the mailbox anymore."

April giggled. Wil's excitement was contagious. If only Wil could be in as good a mood more often, life would be much easier. "That's a great idea!" April said, then frowned. "But how are you going to fake a letter from USC? Don't we need their letterhead and stuff?"

"If it's letterhead you want . . ." Wil said easily, right-clicking on the USC logo. "Letterhead you shall have." She opened a new Word document and right-clicked again, the red-and-gold USC logo appearing on the blank page. She grinned up at April, proud of her work. "I found the head coach's name online, too."

"Brilliant!" April said, amazed.

"Thanks," Wil answered modestly, tapping her sneaker against the table leg. "I've been faking letters for a number of years now." Wil dated the letter and addressed it to Colin in care of Wellness Canyon. "'Dear Mr. Brady,'" she read as she typed. "'We regret to inform you of our decision to not accept you into our football program because of our strict weight-limit requirements—,'" Wil said.

April giggled.

Wil stared at the computer screen, thinking. "How about this—'We don't have any jockstraps in your small size?'" Wil asked.

April laughed loudly, covering her mouth.

"Too much?" Wil asked.

"Yeah." April giggled at the thought of Colin opening the letter excitedly and reading their words, his heart falling at each one. But she didn't feel even one ounce of pity for him—not after the way he'd said to her, *You're sort of sitting in someone's seat*, as if he were the coolest person on the planet and she was nobody at all. He deserved whatever he got in return. "He'll know it's us."

Wil sighed. "Yeah, okay." She deleted the jockstrap bit and finished typing the letter. They spent fifteen minutes trying to un-jam the color printer, Wil having sent two envelopes through at once, and April began to lose her nerve.

"Come on!" April felt the flutter of butterflies in her stomach as they hunted for Colin, the ink hardly dry on their letter. She couldn't wait to see the look on Colin's face when his beloved USC turned him down; she hoped it stung as badly as what he'd done to her in the dining hall.

"We'll go slip it into his mailbox in the Lodge," Wil said. April followed her to down the pebbled path from the computer lab to the Lodge, giddy with excitement. They were almost there, when they suddenly heard Gregg's loud voice from the nearby spa building. "Dude, that's unbelievable." Gregg said. Wil held up her hand and they crouched down and snuck around to where the hot tub was out back. April peeked around a tree trunk and could just see Colin, Gregg, and the Barely Chubbies all sitting around the hot tub. Everyone's attention was on Colin.

"Yeah," Colin said, his voice full of pride. "Just got the letter today. I guess Coach misaddressed it or something. He said that not only will USC be scouting me at homecoming, but most of the big ten schools will be there too."

Wil slowly turned to look at April, looking about as disappointed as April felt. Wil muttered something unintelligible and crumpled the letter in her hand. She spun around and stalked away. April was on her heels, eager to hear plan B.

# CHAPTER 23

**DATE:** July 25th

**FOOD:** Nothing. And I'm famished.

**EXERCISE:** Not really anything besides Colin's stupid letter—but I'm surprisingly exhausted.

"IT *WAS* A GREAT IDEA," APRIL ADMITTED, SOUNDING LIKE SHE wanted to cheer Wil up.

"Doesn't matter now, though, right?" Wil stomped ahead of April as they made their way back to Franklin. She'd been so sure the letter would cause Colin's ultimate humiliation, she'd predicted he'd pack his stuff in the middle of the night and just leave. The plan was so good that she'd replayed it in her mind over and over, like watching it on TiVo. The fact that it had been completely foiled and he would now act even *more* arrogant only made it worse.

"What's that?" April asked, pointing to the box outside their door. She leaned over and read the label, gingerly picking up the package as if it were a bomb that might explode. "It's from your parents," she said, handing the box to Wil. "It's light."

Wil recognized her mother's scrawl on the address label and saw a note from Melanie: *Package has been at mail center for five days. Was going to be thrown away.* "Better not be another blueprint," she muttered as April unlocked their door.

"What?" April asked, stepping inside the room behind Wil.

"Nothing." Wil pocketed the note from Melanie and set the box on her bed, a little afraid of what was inside. There was no way the package contained anything good, like, say, a new stash of Godiva to make up for the one she had gorged herself on after Colin completely embarrassed her in the dining hall. Once, when Wil had spent two weeks at her cousin's house in Kansas City, her parents had sent a care package full of vitamins, wrist and ankle weights, and protein powder. Wil shuddered.

"Are you going to open it?" April asked, peeking over Wil's shoulder. "Maybe it's your edible flowerpot."

"My parents aren't that clever." Wil said, looking at April quizzically. "Hey, why are you doing your own laundry? We all sent it out yesterday," she said as she sat down on her bed.

"Oh, I don't know," April replied, smiling and looking a little distracted. "I just didn't want to wait for it to come back, I guess."

"Whatever," Wil said as she pulled the box onto her lap. "Hey, can you help me for a minute?" April went over and steadied the package while Wil ripped into it. A layer of pink tissue paper obscured whatever the box held and Wil quickly tore it away—anything wrapped in pink tissue paper could *not* be good.

"What is it?" April asked, leaning over the box.

Wil pulled out the contents one by one and dropped them into a near pile on her bed. A light pink fitted T-shirt that read JUICY COUTURE in gothic white script, a plum-colored Adidas by Stella McCartney tennis skirt that looked like it was barely long enough to cover her butt, a couple of Danskin stretchy tank tops, although Wil hadn't owned a tank top since she was eight. And they were all at least five sizes too small. Wil turned the box upside down and a few more articles of clothing fell out.

April reached into the box and held up a hot pink Adidas sports bra with the word SEXY emblazoned across the front in rhinestones. She snickered a little and grinned sheepishly at Wil. "Wow, your parents *reallllly* don't get you, huh?" She tossed the sports bra on the bed and picked out a white L.A.M.B. hoodie with a pink diagonal stripe across it and matching flared yoga pants. "Those are nice, though."

"Then they're all yours." Wil pushed the box away. Her stomach hurt from the thought that her parents had actually stood in Saks and picked this tiny stuff out for her, as if they just couldn't wait until she was eight sizes smaller. "Take whatever you want."

April picked up the Adidas sports bra hesitantly. "Yeah?"

"Seriously." Wil didn't want any of it.

# CHAPTER 24

**DATE:** July 28th

**FOOD:** 3 whole-wheat pancakes with flax and baked apples. Surprisingly, not that bad

**EXERCISE:** Some weights. Had to prepare for the rowing competition somehow

JUST AS WIL HAD PREDICTED, COLIN'S AGGRESSIVE JOCKINESS HAD gotten worse. On the morning of the Wellness Canyon rowing competition, he jumped into his team's boat shouting, "Think Michigan will like this move?" loud enough for the entire camp to hear. His teammates giggled, Gregg included, as the boat teetered a little in the water before straightening up.

"You'd think he wouldn't want to jinx it," Wil grumbled, letting her fingers trail in the cool water of Lake Jennings.

"This morning I saw him practicing an end-zone dance," April said to Wil. "I'd show you, but I think the hip gyrating would probably tip us."

Their seats were in the front, next to each other, two bucket seats that slid to give their legs a full workout too. Their boat bobbed up and down as Dave and Paul got in and strapped themselves into the seats behind April and Wil. Wil thunked her oar into the water, sending a splash of water in the air. A light breeze blew, sending the little droplets onto April.

"It's just sickening." Wil glanced over at Colin and Gregg. They were reaching over the side of their boat to splash Jessica and Marci, who could apparently do nothing but giggle at them.

"Eyes forward," Melanie barked into her megaphone. She stood near the end of the wooded dock that jutted out into the water. "Here's how it'll work," she bellowed, walking up and down the dock as she spoke. "All twenty-five boats will take a practice lap around the lake to get you used to the strokes we just showed you. Then we'll have the relay heats. This will be the starting point. So row around once and stop when you get back here." Melanie pointed at the dock emphatically.

"Ready, ladies?" Paul called from the back as he pushed off with his oar.

"I've never rowed before," April admitted. "Not even on the rowing machine in the gym."

"Just don't plunge your oar down into the water," Paul said. "Or it'll stop the boat or turn it sharply." He laughed. "Or tip us over."

"We're just going straight out and back," Dave told April reassuringly. "So you should be fine. Just try to find a rhythm."

"Let's go," Wil said, irritated at the sight of all the other boats ahead of them. "We're behind already." She looked over at

Colin's boat, cruising out into the water. All four of the boat's passengers were laughing as Colin plunked his oar down into the water, spraying everyone.

"This isn't the race part," Dave reminded her.

The warm morning sun beat down on their skin as they rowed together. The lake was much bluer than Wil had expected, and the water smelled surprisingly fresh and clean. She tried to concentrate on something, anything—the beautiful day, the soothing sound the oars made when they sliced into the water, the cool breeze tickling her nose—but every three seconds she was distracted by Colin whooping and yelling ahead of them.

"We need a plan B," Wil reminded April, nodding in Colin's direction as his boat glided easily through the water.

"I know." April lowered her voice. "ASAP."

"I was thinking I could bribe someone who works for my parents' club to pretend to be a sports trainer from USC or some other school to come up and give Colin a physical. And then the trainer could tell Colin he's too fat." Wil gripped her oar tightly with both hands as she rowed.

"That would be hilarious," April replied. "But it sounds kind of complicated."

"Yeah." Wil glanced over her shoulder at Dave and Paul and smiled. She could hear them talking about which Tom Cruise movie they hated the most—which might have been an interesting conversation if Wil hadn't been so preoccupied with beating Colin in this non-race. "Plus, no one who works for my parents likes me enough to do it. Or likes me at all, I should say."

"What about something like putting Saran Wrap across his toilet?" April asked. "I heard that works pretty well."

"Not public enough." Wil shook her head, pulling the oar through the water.

"Let's pick up the pace, ladies," Paul called out. "Or we're going to be last!"

Wil turned around and good-naturedly stuck out her tongue at him. "We're saving it for the race."

Wil skimmed the surface of the water with her oar, syncing her stroke with April's. They were more than halfway around the lake and a breeze picked up, propelling them toward Melanie and her megaphone. "Well, I can't think of anything else. I just want to make it good," April said, glaring at Colin's boat.

"Don't worry. I'll come up with something," Wil promised.

They guided their boat back toward the shore—the second-to-last boat to dock—and listened to Melanie's instructions about the relay heats. "Kevin is on the other shoreline to make sure you touch."

Wil, April, Dave, and Paul were in the first heat, lined up with three other boats. Two of them held campers that Wil and April had barely talked to, but the boat directly next to them held Colin's team. Just over a week had passed since their kiss and Wil *still* hadn't exacted her revenge on him. It was driving her nuts. And she knew that it was driving April crazy too.

"Row!" Melanie yelled, lifting both hands in the air.

"Let's go," Wil called back to Paul and Dave, who fired up their strokes, sending the boat a full length ahead of the nearest team—Colin's. Colin, Gregg, Jessica, and Marci were followed by a boat containing four girls who only talked to each other, and in last place was a fourth boat piloted by the guy who was always first in line in the dining hall. Wil dipped her oar in the water, pulling toward her chest with all her might, her muscles flexing with each stroke. She looked over at Colin and threw herself into rowing.

Kevin stood on the far shore, holding a yellow flag over his head. Wil and April steered right toward him, the wind rustling Wil's curls. "Touch!" Kevin yelled as their boat ran aground.

"Push off!" Paul yelled.

Wil and April dug their oars into the rocky shoreline and pushed, but the boat didn't move.

"Come on!" Wil cried. They had been making such good time—good enough to beat Colin! She didn't want to lose that now.

"Harder!" Paul shouted.

"Touch!" Kevin called out as the next boat reached the shore.

Wil felt like she was straining every muscle in her body as she leaned on her oar, but she didn't let up until she finally felt the boat starting to float backward. "C'mon!" she screamed, her face turning red.

"And turn!" Dave called out, his voice ringing through the clear air.

"That's you," Wil told April. "Put your oar in and try to fight the water back." April did as Wil instructed and she and Dave turned the boat around.

"Touch!" Kevin yelled, Colin's team's boat reaching the shore.

"Woo-hoo!" Gregg shouted as his teammates started to cheer.

"Ha ha, *suckas*!" Colin called over to their boat. Wil clutched her oar tighter and glared.

"Come on, we gotta go!" Wil called over her shoulder, ignoring the twitch in her biceps. She didn't relax her grip.

Paul and Dave took two long pulls on their oars and Wil and April synced their strokes again. Colin's boat easily skimmed ahead of them as sweat began to pour from Wil's forehead. She imagined Colin mocking her from his boat's stern and she pushed harder, blocking out everything but the rhythm of her oar smacking down into the lake.

"I can't make it," April said suddenly, panting and holding her oar slightly out of the water.

Wil looked over but didn't stop rowing. She noticed the front of April's shirt soaked through with sweat. At the same time, though, Wil realized that April looked pretty and suddenly very small. Wil could see April's arm muscles flex as she rowed. For the first time, Wil realized just how much weight April had lost. "You *can* make it," Wil said encouragingly. She tried to row harder to make up for April. "We're almost there."

Colin's boat pulled a full length ahead of theirs and took over the lead as Melanie's features slowly became more defined in their field of vision. As hard as Wil tried, she felt their boat slow down from April's tired strokes. The other campers cheered, screamed, and clapped from the shore as Colin's team pulled into the dock and Melanie blew her whistle. Paul and Dave eased up, their boat cruising to an easy second as Wil watched Colin, Gregg, Jessica, and Marci jump up and down on the dock.

"Oh man!" Paul splashed his oar into the water. "We almost had it."

"I'm sorry." April's face had fallen, and she looked miserable as she climbed out of the boat and onto the dock.

Wil couldn't believe that her chance to beat Colin had been squandered in a few short seconds. "We were so close!" The four teammates walked slowly away from the dock to deposit their oars and life jackets in a pile for the next heat.

"Wil, it'll be okay," April suggested, looking at Wil.

Wil threw her life jacket on the pile and sighed loudly. "I know. It's just . . . well. We were just so close." Wil repeated, not knowing what to say. She couldn't wait to get her revenge on Colin. Nothing else would make her feel better.

# CHAPTER 25

**DATE:** July 31st

**FOOD:** Veggie burger on whole-wheat bun with lettuce and tomato. Actually edible.

**EXERCISE:** Nothing since rowing. My arms just <u>ache</u>.

DESPITE THE BEST EFFORTS OF APRIL AND MELANIE, WIL HAD ONLY been to the gym two other times throughout the whole summer. The first time, she managed five minutes on the treadmill before she gave up and decided that it was mind-numbingly boring. The second time, she tried a yoga class and was so embarrassed that she couldn't do three-quarters of the poses that she gave up and never came back. Melanie had given her another demerit for not showing up for her training, but she eventually gave up. Wil was relieved. She figured the daily camp activities were enough "activity" for anyone.

Wil walked into the open, airy Pilates/spinning/yoga studio and was about to turn around—she was looking for a punching bag to hit—when she spied Colin perched on a stationary bike next to Jessica. The two of them were pedaling casually and chatting as if they were a couple just out for a ride in the park. Wil looked around at the full room and noticed that the only free bike was in the row directly behind them. A bunch of other campers were standing around stretching and talking before the class began, their sweatshirts and water bottles claiming their spots.

"I'm up to ten one-armed push-ups," Colin bragged to Jessica, flexing his right bicep for her. He was, of course, wearing a sleeveless T-shirt—one that looked like he'd ripped the sleeves off himself.

"Pretty good," Jessica said, her silky blond ponytail wagging like an excited dog's tail.

Wil saw Colin do a double take out of the corner of her eye, and she pretended to study the room.

"Hey, pork chop," Colin said quietly over his shoulder to Wil. "Try the back. It's cooler there." Wil shot him a poisonous look, but he just turned back to Jessica. Wil searched her mind for the perfect comeback, one that would sink into Colin's rotten core and stab him in his black heart, but her mind was blank. And besides, he would probably just ignore her, anyway. She was about to go off in search of the punching bag—which she could *really* use now—but part of her wanted to show up Colin and Jessica and everyone else who was at Wellness Canyon but still looked down on the fat kids.

"Ready, cyclers?" the instructor, a ridiculously fit woman named Heidi, asked as she entered the room and mounted the bike at the front of the class. The instructor fitted the yellow sport wireless headset microphone over her head and fiddled with the stack of components on her left. "Testing, one, two, three." Her breathy voice blared from the Bose speakers recessed all around them.

Wil stared at Colin's back, squinting a laser beam of white-hot hate that she hoped he could feel. She walked over to the cycle directly behind him and got on, adjusting the height and resistance. The crash of "Independent Woman" pumped through the speakers for the warm-up, and everyone started cycling. Wil cranked the pedals slowly, shifting in her seat. She flashed back to the one other time she'd been on a stationary bike. It had been at her parents' first club, and her mother had stood over her and shouting encouragement as she tried to ride. Wil's legs had been too short to really pump the pedals like the other cyclists, who all looked on, amused. She'd been embarrassed, even then.

"Everyone set their bikes to program seven," Heidi instructed, her head bobbing as her pedals whirled. "We're doing a little mountain biking today."

*Hey, pork chop.* Wil slammed down on the pedals, initiating the program with the touch of a button. A series of digital peaks and valleys appeared on the red display panel and Wil focused on the counter as her step total multiplied by two. She peered ahead at Colin's counter and saw that he was sixty or so steps ahead of her. *I can see now why your parents are so embarrassed of you.* She picked up her pedal stroke, gaining on Colin, who laced his hands behind his head and sat straight up, exhaling loudly. As everyone hit the first hill, the music sped up to keep them in time.

Jessica rose and leaned her elbows on the armrests and Wil did the same, increasing her pedaling speed. She could see that she was neck and neck with Jessica's pedal count and she sped up, her feet whirling around like a cyclone until her count was a dozen or more ahead of Jessica's. She was surprised by her own stamina.

*Hey, pork chop. I can see now why your parents are so embarrassed of you.*

Wil cranked up the resistance on her bike, Lance Armstrong–style, as the digital display indicated a long plateau. Not only would she beat Colin, but she'd do it with more resistance. Her legs threatened to cramp, but Wil pushed ahead. Her whole body swayed and she stood up, now riding the bike past Colin on the imaginary plateau. She didn't look back as she left him to choke on her dust, wishing that she hadn't wasted so much of her time thinking about such a jerk. The music pumped louder and Heidi kept shouting, "You can do it! Harder. Faster. Go, go, go!" and Wil answered the call as the other campers struggled around her. She disengaged entirely, her body on autopilot as she floated above, peering down on Colin's measly pedal count, the fires of resentment burning inside her brain. *I can see now why your parents are so embarrassed of you.* Wil pushed herself harder, putting all of her fiery anger into kicking Colin's butt.

"Great job, Wil!" Heidi exclaimed over the loudspeaker as the music slowed back down. Everyone looked over at her and she couldn't help but beam. Not only at beating Colin, but also for pushing herself. She was shocked. She actually felt *good*.

# CHAPTER 26

**DATE:** August 1st

**FOOD:** Large spinach salad with tomatoes, ¼ avocado, and ⅓ c. chickpeas

**EXERCISE:** 6 sets of leg lifts on each side and 45 crunches!

"HE SAID *THAT*?" APRIL ASKED INCREDULOUSLY, LISTENING TO Wil's story about Colin at yesterday's spinning session. "Unbelievable."

April and Wil were stretching their legs in the cool shade of the Lodge, as they stood with a large group of campers who were waiting for the power-walk to start. Other campers straggled out of the dining hall and headed back to their dorms to get in an afternoon nap. The post-lunch power walk had been made voluntary after a girl from Oregon sprayed the Wellness Canyon driveway with regurgitated fat-free ricotta cheese lasagna a few weeks ago.

"The funny thing," Wil continued, taking a bite of an apple she picked up on her way out of the dining hall, "is that he's not

162

even really that good-looking. I can name five guys from my high school that are better-looking than Colin. I can't believe I ever liked him. He's so . . . gross."

"Did you ever notice that he smells like b.o. *all* the time?" April giggled. "I mean, I know he works out a lot, but still." April still didn't consider Wil a good friend, exactly—and she still wouldn't tell her the truth about not having any money— but they'd spent so much time together and were so aligned against the common enemy that it felt like April could at least consider her an ally.

"And he tries to cover it up with that awful cologne." Wil bent down to pull up her socks. "Gross."

April and Wil let a group of other campers pass them. They brought up the rear as the pack made its way down the long driveway toward the front gates. "I can't believe I actually kissed him." April shuddered in disgust. "Ugh. It makes me want to throw up." At the time, she'd thought her first kiss was going to be the one she remembered all her life, but now she just wished she could forget it ever happened.

A faraway look came across Wil's face and she kicked some pebbles down the long, gravelly driveway. "I had this fabulous dream the other night that Colin broke his leg running after his stupid Frisbee on the lawn and I ran over with the others to help him. Then, in the middle of the dream, I heard my own voice saying, 'What are you doing? You don't care if his leg is broken.'" Wil peered at the sky, which was clouding over for once. "It was weird."

"If only," April said, not really meaning it. She didn't really want Colin to break any bones. She just wanted him—for once in his perfect, football-playing popular-guy life—to realize what it felt like to be humiliated, to have everyone stare at you and snicker and know that they were going to keep talking about you behind your back. "Hey. Let's do an extra lap today," April said to Wil. "We have to brainstorm anyway; we might as well burn calories at the same time."

"Whatever," Wil said, hiking up her sagging black soccer shorts as they approached the end of the long driveway. Even if Wil didn't want to admit it, April noticed that Wil had lost some weight. "I'm still mad about the letter. It was a genius idea. I just want to get him so bad."

"What about the idea you were talking about the other day? Taking all his clothes and hiding them at Huge Rock?" April pulled the elastic out of her hair and shook out her ponytail. She was wearing a turquoise Fila tank top from Wil's parents' care package. "That would be funny. He'd have to run around naked looking for his clothes."

"Nah, he'd probably enjoy that too much." Wil snorted. "He'd *love* the idea that someone wanted to see him naked."

"Gross." April hadn't actually pictured Colin running naked across Wellness Canyon. "What about catching a lizard and putting it in his room?"

"Or what about a rattlesnake?" Wil's blue eyes grew wide. "It could bite him right on his you-know-what."

April shrieked with laughter and the other campers turned

to look. Wil and April waited as a group crossed the street and hit the wooded trail, a couple of tired campers just coming back up the driveway toward the Lodge. While all of the campers were looking better than they had when they arrived, April could tell that some were getting worn down from the daily exercises and competitions.

April's body was sore, but she was more energized than she'd ever been before. She could tell from the way she wasn't getting winded as easily that she wasn't just losing weight, but actually getting in shape.

"How could we catch a rattlesnake?" April asked, returning suddenly to the moment. "Wouldn't it bite us?"

Wil shrugged. "Maybe." The two of them headed onto the wooded trail. Once in the woods, the power walkers broke off down different trails, and April was reminded of that day way back in the beginning when she and Wil had gotten lost. "But it doesn't hurt. I heard about this kid once that got bit by a rattlesnake in Malibu and he was, like, fine the next day. They just took him to the hospital and gave him a shot of anti-venom."

"Hmmm . . . it seems like it would hurt," April said doubtfully, slapping a bug away from her arm. It sounded awfully serious to her.

"I'll bet there are a lot of rattlesnakes up on Huge Rock," Wil said, thinking aloud. Branches crunched beneath her feet. "We'd need like a pillowcase or something."

The thought of sneaking around up at Huge Rock in the middle of the night, carrying a pillowcase and trying to attract a rattlesnake, freaked April out. "Maybe we could get the cook to slip something into his food," she said, trying to change the subject.

Wil clutched April's bare arm and they both stopped in the middle of the trail. There were no other campers in sight. "Oh my God! That's brilliant!" Wil's eyes lit up and she headed off the trail, breaking into a jog.

"What? What did I say?" April yelled after her, trying to catch up. She was still ten feet behind Wil when she stepped through an opening in the brush and into the 7-Eleven parking lot, empty except for a cop car. She slowed down at the sight of the cruiser, worried that the cop would somehow know that they were doing something they weren't supposed to. But Wil breezed past the officer and into the store as if nothing was up and April followed her lead. The cop looked at April—he was actually kind of young and cute—and smiled. April smiled back, hanging her head a little as she walked by. Then the police radio stole the officer's attention, and he hopped into his car and sped off.

April walked in the door and rounded the candy aisle, expecting to find Wil with a handful of candy bars and Reese's peanut butter cups, but the aisle was empty. April stared for a moment at a bag of Hershey's Kisses. The shiny foil wrapping called out to her like twinkling stars, and she actually reached out to touch them. But she liked the new way her clothes were starting to feel—even the smaller sizes she had brought were getting a little loose—and so she forced herself to look away. She concentrated instead on her surprisingly small image in the tiny security monitor in the front corner of the store. "Over here," Wil's voice called out from behind a display of potato chip bags. April saw her waving on the monitor too.

"If Melanie busts us again, she'll have a hernia," April said, poking her head around the corner. She wouldn't even let herself glance and see if they had Cheetos.

"Whatever." Wil rolled her eyes.

April stared at Wil, who didn't seem to be paying attention to the chips either. "What are you getting?"

"Voila!" Wil said, sweeping her hand across the shelfful of laxatives. "Help me grab these," she said, grabbing boxes of extra-strength Ex-Lax.

"Why do you want laxatives?" April asked. "We're not allowed to have them here. It's one of the things Melanie said was banned on the—"

Wil cut her off, waving a box of Fibercon in front of her eyes. "They're not for us, silly."

A flash of understanding hit April. "Ohhhhh . . ." She snatched a box of Citrucel from its hook and examined it. "But these are pills. How can we fool Colin into taking them?"

"We'll crush them up and mix them into his protein powder," Wil said gleefully as she led April to the front counter.

The cashier, a woman with streaked blond hair and bored eyes, looked Wil and April up and down as they loaded the laxatives onto the counter. "Everything okay?" she asked, picking up the first box.

"Yeah," Wil said nonchalantly, as if she bought laxatives in bulk all the time. She pulled a wad of money out of her sock.

"This is going to be like fifty bucks," April whispered to her.

"A worthy investment." Wil unwrapped the credit card at the center of her roll of ones and fives.

"Cool," April said, admiring the gold American Express. "Is that yours?"

"Of course. Don't you have one?" Wil said as she plunked it down on the counter.

"Oh, my mom wants me to wait. Until I'm eighteen. Totally lame, right?" April giggled nervously, hoping that Wil wouldn't press the issue. She'd tried to get her mother to co-sign for a credit card so she could pay for Wellness Springs, but her mother said her credit wasn't good enough to co-sign for a ham sandwich.

"Forty-seven fifty," the cashier announced. She glanced at the small digital clock to her left. She looked like she couldn't wait until her shift was over and she didn't have to deal with laxative-buying fat campers anymore.

"I assume you want a bag," the cashier said after Wil had signed the receipt.

"No thanks," Wil said, scooping the laxatives into her arms. April followed her out the door and to the sticky picnic table in the parking lot. Wil methodically went about breaking the pills and packets of powder free of their cumbersome cardboard boxes and handing half of them to April. April felt like a kid as she and Wil stuffed the pills into the toes and sides of their shoes.

"Ready?" Wil asked, standing up.

April felt a cracking sensation as she stood. "I think I broke some," she said.

"Doesn't matter," Wil said, still smiling. "We'll have to crush them up anyway. I hope your feet are sweaty."

April smiled back at Wil and felt the satisfying crunch of the pills beneath her feet.

# CHAPTER 27

**DATE:** August 3rd

**FOOD:** Suddenly and surprisingly not hungry

**EXERCISE:** Lots of power-walking and another exercise session with Dave—we really keep each other motivated!

"GOD, I'M BORED," WIL MOANED. APRIL AND WIL WERE HANGING out in their room after dinner and April was reading a book that Melanie had loaned her on whole foods nutrition. She'd thought it had to do with the organic grocery store chain before she started, but as it turned out, it was completely fascinating. So many things about Wellness Canyon weren't what she had expected.

"So watch a show on your iPod," April offered nonchalantly. She knew Wil had about fifty TV shows on the thing.

"I've watched everything twice," Wil whined, swinging around on the bed so that she was hanging upside down. "What does everyone else do around here at night?"

"Seriously? They all hang out over at the Lodge. Every night. You didn't know that?" April asked, putting down her book and looking at Wil incredulously.

"Really? Want to go over?" Wil said, righting herself on the bed again. April watched as Wil got up and put on her sweatshirt, looking at April expectantly.

"Yeah, sure," April agreed, surprised at her response. The first time had been a bust, but with Wil over there too, at least she would have someone to talk to. "Anyway, I think I heard Dave and Paul talking about heading over there tonight."

The girls shut the door to their room and headed down the lantern-lit path toward the Lodge. As they approached the large porch, they could hear laughter and talking and April smiled at how homey the building looked, brightly lit and bustling.

Wil and April entered the wide double doors and made their way into the lobby, where other campers were playing games and watching a movie.

"April!" April whirled around at the voice and smiled when she saw Paul and Dave over by the pool table, already pretty far into their game.

"Hey." April and Wil walked over to the guys and sat down on two of the large bar stools surrounding the table.

Suddenly, the phone rang, startling April and causing Paul to miss the cue ball completely.

"Hello?" Wil reached for the phone, clearly excited by this new development. "Who is this?" she asked suspiciously.

The Lodge phone had been a source of practical jokes lately—April had heard that someone had called pretending to be from the city council with a complaint that the campers were polluting Lake Jennings, and April looked over, anticipating a joke.

"Oh yeah, sure," Wil said. "Just a second." She cupped the receiver and called to April. "It's your mom," Wil whispered. "Good timing, eh?"

April's eyes grew wide as she took up the phone. "Mom?" April asked in a low voice, turning toward the wall. April was suddenly nervous. After getting her care package a few weeks ago, she hadn't called her mom once. It just seemed so unfair that everyone else at Wellness Canyon had parents who wanted them to be here—who had even paid for them to come—and what had April's mom done? Sent her cookies. And April was pretty sure they had trans fats in them, which were super-bad, according to her book. "How are you?"

"Hi, sweetie," April's mom said easily, not answering her question. "How are you doing?"

"I'm good! I still really love it here and everything's going great with my roommate. Oh! And Melanie let me borrow this really interesting book. I'll have to tell you all about it." April began making some uncomfortable small talk. These few weeks had been the longest she hadn't talked to her mom, and she just wanted to pretend it was normal—especially with so many people around to listen in.

"That's good, honey. Look Apie, I'm sorry to do this over the phone, but I have to tell you something," her mother interrupted. April could sense tension in her mom's voice. Plus, she had called her "Apie"—a nickname April hadn't had for years—so she knew that something must have been wrong.

"Is everything okay?" April looked over at the pool table, where Paul was clubbing Dave with the end of his pool cue.

"Sweetheart, I went to Dr. Tighe today," she began. April eased herself onto the stool, using the wall for support. She knew that whatever the news was, it couldn't be good. "I have diabetes."

"Oh my God, Mom . . ." April's heart sped up as she turned to face the wall. She only half-listened as her mom continued on about her dietary restrictions and daily injections. Her mom had never really been good about taking care of herself. April had worried about her mom before—but then it was just about bad food decisions. What about now that it was so important? April was learning so much about health, diet, and exercise this summer—stuff that her mom had no way of knowing. How would her mom handle all of that by herself?

"Really, honey, I'm fine. Things might be a little tricky right now getting used to the insulin shots, but I think it will be okay. They're not talking about anything serious yet." April's mother tried to sound comforting, but April could hear the fear in her voice.

"Mom, I think that I should come home. You shouldn't do this on your own," April suggested, twirling the phone cord around her fingers.

"No, honey, you waited all year for this. You have to stay," her mother insisted. April heard Cleo, their cat, meowing on the other end of the line.

April sniffled and knew that Wil, Dave, and Paul could

probably hear everything she was saying, but she didn't care. Hot tears crept up in her eyes and she concentrated on not sobbing.

"It's okay, sweetie," her mom said. Now April could hear her mother start to cry. "Apie, I don't want you to end up like me," she began, sounding strained. "You have to stay. You have to beat this. Even if I can't."

"Oh, Mom," April said, bursting into tears. She turned her back to the room and leaned forward on the stool, resting her head against the cool plaster on the wall.

"It's okay, honey. Everything's really going to be okay. You'll be home in no time. You make me so proud, honey." April's mother was crying now. "I love you."

"I love you, Mom." April hung up the phone and stared at the wall. She felt so helpless, yet she knew that her mother was right—she had to stay here. She had to do this. For herself and for her mom.

# CHAPTER 28

**DATE:** *August 5th*

**FOOD:** *1 hummus-and-fresh-vegetable whole wheat wrap and ½ c. grapes*

**EXERCISE:** *Weights and cardio with trainer*

A FEW DAYS LATER, APRIL WAS ON THE LAWN, WAITING WITH the rest of the campers for the afternoon competition to begin. This was the last competition leading up to the end-of-summer Olympics, and everyone was feeling just a little nervous.

April wiped the sweat from her brow with the back of her hand. The lawn was covered in sunlight and there was no shade anywhere. "Okay, teams," Melanie instructed. "Line up." April took her post near a bin of odd-looking watermelons. Wil paced off three steps next to her, Dave next to Wil, and Paul at the other end, near the empty bin. All across the lawn, the rest of the teams did the same.

Melanie explained the competition: each bin held ten watermelons smeared in Crisco. Each team was to pass the watermelons one at a time to their teammates; the last in line would deposit the watermelon in the empty bin. Any dropped watermelon stayed on the ground. Whichever team transferred the most watermelons in five minutes won.

"Are you sure you don't want to switch places with me?" Wil asked, fanning herself. "My arms are a little longer."

April peered into the deep bin at the slick watermelons. The sides of the bin had been slicked with Crisco too. "I can reach," she said. Since the upsetting conversation with her mother earlier in the week, April felt motivated to try even harder, which was why she volunteered to be the one to scoop the watermelons out of the bin.

"Remember to hand it," Dave said under his breath. "If you throw it or pull away too fast, it'll drop to the ground. That's the trick."

April nodded. She wiped her hands on her shorts to dry them off. She looked over her shoulder and noticed Colin staring at her. He grinned.

"Ready?" Melanie called out.

"Ready!" The campers shouted back. Colin's voice carried over all of them, his eyes still on April.

"Start!" Melanie yelled.

April bent over and reached into the bin, her fingertips scraping the top of the first watermelon. She scooped her hands under the greasy fruit and hoisted it out like an overweight baby, fumbling several times before she dropped it safely into Wil's outstretched arms.

"Got it," Wil said, her face scrunched up in concentration.

Wil walked over to Dave with care and handed the watermelon off to him. It wobbled a little and slid into his arms.

"Got it," Dave said. He waddled over to Paul.

"Got it," Paul said as he took the watermelon from Dave. He carefully lowered it into the bin.

As April reached into the bin, she could hear campers all across the lawn shouting encouragement to their teammates. She moved toward Wil, but as she did, she felt the watermelon sliding out of her hands. She tried to push it over to Wil, who seemed to be an extra step away.

"No, no, no!" Wil cried as she crashed into April, the watermelon taking a high bounce off the lawn until it came down and broke in two.

"Sucks to be you," Colin called from behind them as Marci dropped a watermelon into their bin.

Burning with anger, April immediately fished out another watermelon, more carefully this time. The watermelon traveled successfully the whole way to Paul again, who slipped it triumphantly into the bin at the other end. A thin layer of grease coated April's hands, but Melanie said that anyone caught wiping grease off their hands would be disqualified, so April resisted smearing the white goo on her shorts.

Dave dropped a watermelon handoff from Wil, who called out, "Butterfingers!" and then laughed. "I *wish* I had a Butterfinger right now."

April thought it was pretty funny, though, since the last time they had been at the 7-Eleven, Wil hadn't even glanced at the candy.

"How many?" Dave asked after handing another watermelon successfully to Paul.

"Seven," Paul called out. "C'mon, April, give us another!"

"How many?" Colin yelled down to Marci, next to them.

"Seven," Marci yelled back.

April looked at the remaining three watermelons. They'd need all ten to win, probably, having dropped two already. They were neck and neck with Colin's team. She reached into the bin, trying not to think about how disgusting it felt to have her arms covered in grease. She carefully brought up the next watermelon, which was almost white with Crisco.

"Steady," Wil advised. She held out her grease-slicked arms, her elbows anchored into her stomach to catch the load.

"Forty-five seconds," Melanie called out from the Lodge porch.

Wil turned and hefted the watermelon to Dave, who successfully passed it to Paul. April noticed Colin skimming his hands over the top of the bin to remove some of the excess grease. She shook it off and confidently reached in for the second-to-last watermelon, which was unexpectedly light. She watched as the watermelon popped up and sailed in slow motion to her right, landing near Kevin and rolling under one of the bushes lining the lawn.

"Keep going, April!" Wil said just as Jessica cried out, her watermelon splattering on the ground.

April carefully passed the final watermelon. She prayed for it not to wobble out of her tired arms. Once she handed it safely off to Wil, she watched the rest of the scene, almost in slow motion. Wil passed it to Dave and then Dave passed it to Paul, who dropped it into the bin. April's focus drifted as she watched Jessica make a similar handoff to Marci, the last watermelon coming right behind the previous one. Marci deposited them both into the bin and raised her arms like a runner crossing the finish line.

"Time!" Melanie called. She blew a whistle, startling everyone. One of the chubby girls at the far end of the lawn dropped a watermelon right as she was about to deposit it into her team's bin. "Count, please."

Kevin, Cammie, and some of the other counselors circled the bins and counted the watermelons. April wiped the grease off her hands on the top of the bin, staring at Colin as she did. "Oh, good idea," he said, dramatically wiping the grease from his hands the same way he had before. April narrowed her eyes.

The counselors conferred for a moment and everyone was hushed, waiting. All of a sudden Kevin pointed at April, Wil, Dave, and Paul and shouted, "Winners!"

"Yes!" Dave pumped his fist in the air. He and Paul exchanged a greasy high five as Kevin called out second place for Colin's team, and third went to the all-girl team, who seemed happy just to have placed.

"Nice work," Wil said to April, grinning. April smiled back. She couldn't remember having come in first place in anything before—ever.

"Go, team!" Paul said, holding his hand out. Dave put his

hand on top of Paul's, and Wil and April followed suit. They let out a giant roar as they all lifted their hands into the air.

"We might just have a chance yet!" April cried, the euphoria of winning starting to sink in.

"Damn right." Wil met April's eyes, and impulsively, April threw her hand up into the air to meet Wil's. They went in for a strong high five and missed, which knocked them both off balance. Wil and April looked at each other and burst out laughing. Now that they'd won something, it felt like nothing could bring them down.

# CHAPTER 29

**DATE:** August 6th

**FOOD:** 1 hummus-and-fresh-vegetable whole-wheat wrap—April's looked pretty good.

**EXERCISE:** 1-mile swim in the pool

"GOOD MORNING, MISS HOPKINS," MELANIE SAID WHEN WIL showed up for her last weigh-in. The weigh-ins had moved to Melanie's lilac-scented office after a fight broke out at the midsummer weigh-in when one camper called another camper a "lard ass," and the intervening counselor was sent to the infirmary with a bloody nose. When Wil walked in, April was lounging in a chair, clearly pleased with her own weigh-in.

Wil stepped up on the scale and the balance showed a number well short of her previous weight.

"Must be broken." Wil laughed, watching the needle and thinking how strange it was to see it in its current location.

"No," Melanie said, noting the number. "It's working. Wow. Fifteen pounds in two weeks. That's incredible."

Wil stared at the scale.

"That's wonderful!" April shrieked. Before Wil could react, April came at her with her arms open in a celebratory hug.

"Why are you hugging me? It's not like you paid for me to come here," Wil snapped, turning sideways to avoid the hug. She pulled back as April neared, pushing her away when she tried to come in close. April stumbled backward, catching herself against Melanie's too-neat desk, and Wil sat down in the leather chair near the window overlooking the lawn.

April pulled herself together, her pretty face flushed red, and quickly turned and walked out of the office without a word. The door clicked quietly behind her and Wil knew that she was going back to their room to record her weight loss in her food journal and also on the little green weight-loss reminders that the counselors slipped under their doors.

"April just wanted to congratulate you, Wil," Melanie said quietly, her voice reserved and yet somehow full of reproach.

Wil clicked her tongue against the roof her mouth and continued to stare out the window. In the distance, she could see Lake Jennings. A breeze sent tiny ripples along its surface.

"This whole summer, I've been trying to understand why you're so resistant." Melanie took a seat behind her desk. "But for the life of me, I can't. Losing weight is a *good* thing, Wil. That's why you're here."

"Big surprise that *you* think so," Wil barked. Melanie's whole livelihood depended on the fact that rich people were very willing to pay her to take care of their problem-child fat kids.

"What's the big deal?" Melanie asked, scratching her head. Wil thought her face looked green from the bad lighting. "Why can't I think that losing weight is positive?"

"Oh, right." Wil stared at the remnants of black nail polish around her cuticles. "It's not because everyone is so freaking superficial. It's because it's *healthy*. I forgot. Sorry."

"You don't need to be so negative all the time." Melanie shuffled some papers on her desk to indicate that their talk was over, even though she kept talking. "Hundreds of campers have come through Wellness Canyon, so I think it's fair to say that we're not here for the sole purpose of making you suffer. Which means that the only variable to what happens here is you."

Melanie closed a file folder and crossed her arms. "You should try to accept that everyone here—including April, it seems—is invested in you and wants to see you succeed. Why can't you accept that people really might just want to help you?"

Melanie's words made Wil flash back to the horrible day when her parents broke the news about Wellness Canyon to her in the first place. The two of them standing in their matching spandex, holding the sopping carpet, telling her what was for her own good. Wil shuddered.

"You get paid to say that," Wil pointed out.

"Look," Melanie said, raising her voice this time. "If you don't want to lose weight and be healthier, then don't. I can't make you. I really don't care if you ruin this for yourself. But you cannot ruin it for your roommate." Melanie stood up and began to pace her office for emphasis. "You can afford personal trainers and chefs. She can't. Did she tell you she's been saving up for over a year to come here?" Wil's heart sped up immediately. She thought everyone at Wellness Canyon was just like her—spoiled and rich and wanting for nothing. But the idea that April had invested so much time, money, and energy in Wellness Canyon before she had even arrived had never even occurred to Wil, and now she began to sweat.

Wil pictured April putting money in a piggy bank, squirreling away pennies, nickels, and dimes. That was probably going overboard, but what if it wasn't? What must it have been like to save to come here and then get stuck with Wil for a roommate?

"Think about it." Melanie said, leading Wil toward the door. Then Melanie closed the door, leaving Wil alone in the hallway to feel every bit the selfish brat that Melanie had insinuated she was. For once, it seemed Melanie was right.

# CHAPTER 30

**DATE:** August 8th

**FOOD:** Spinach salad with grilled salmon
and cherry tomatoes

**EXERCISE:** Power-walking around camp w/ iPod.
Turns out the Shins make good
workout music . . .

THE NEXT AFTERNOON, WIL FOUND APRIL IN HER USUAL SPOT:
pumping fiercely away on the elliptical machine at the gym.
"Come with me," Wil said, beckoning a sweaty April away from
her workout.

"I'm busy," April said, wiping the sweat off her face with a
small towel. She pressed play on her cracked and taped portable
CD player and turned up the volume. Wil flinched. How could
she have not noticed that her roommate didn't have the same
types of things as everyone else at Wellness Canyon?

"I have a surprise for you," Wil said anxiously, pulling at
her arm. "Please?"

"Fine." April sighed and got down off the machine. She
wiped it clean with antiseptic spray and a paper towel, gathered

her water bottle and sweatshirt, and followed Wil out the door. "What is this about?" April asked, wiping her forehead off with her hoodie.

"Look," Wil began, stopping and looking April briefly in the eyes. "I'm sorry for freaking out on you yesterday. I don't, like, do hugs or whatever. It's totally just not my thing. But I'm sorry. And maybe there's something else I can do. Come on." Wil tugged on April's sleeve and pulled her back toward Franklin.

An hour later, April and Wil were ducked down in a seat at the back of a city bus as it pulled away from the stop closest to Wellness Canyon. A car had been trailing the bus ever since, and the last thing Wil wanted was for Melanie to catch them. Wil peeked up to look.

"Who is it?" April asked, leaning back in her seat and biting her nail nervously.

"Nobody," Wil said, fully sitting up. The thrill of potentially getting busted for a forbidden trip to the mall caused her heart to beat a little faster.

"What do you think would happen if we got caught?" April asked, her brown eyes wide as the bus sped down the back roads. It was clear that she didn't appreciate the excitement that came with transgressive behavior.

"Probably nothing." Wil hadn't even gotten kicked out of camp when she'd been actively trying. But April probably spent her life calculating the odds, trying to balance everyone's perception of her against whether or not she should just go ahead and do what she wanted. "Or who knows—maybe she'd send us home!" Wil added teasingly.

April stuck her tongue out at her. The bus turned onto a busier street and Wil started to see familiar chains: Applebee's, TGI Friday's, Barnes & Noble, the Cheesecake Factory, all seemed to sparkle in the sunlight of suburbia and Wil smiled, satisfied again.

Forty minutes later, the town bus shuddered to a stop at the far end of the nearly empty mall parking lot, and Wil and April disembarked and headed for the entrance. Although Wil normally wouldn't be caught dead in a mall, she was excited to be at this one. She pushed through the double glass doors, holding them open for April, and stepped inside the air-conditioned coolness. "Civilization at last," Wil said, sighing.

"Ahhh . . ." April sniffed the air and took in the scene around her. "I love malls," she confessed. Wil smiled with satisfaction. She'd guessed April felt that way.

Wil stalked over to the illuminated mall directory and examined the floor plan. "So, we're here?" she asked, pointing to a splotch on the map.

"No, silly." April pointed to a different spot on the map. "We just came in here." She looked ahead of her like an explorer who had just discovered a new land. "I think we should start at Macy's—they always have great sales—and then Express, and then 9 West, and then maybe Sephora."

So much for April being nervous. It was suddenly like she was in her element. As April strode in the direction of the posh department store, Wil had to switch to her power-walk pace to keep up. Wil followed April into Macy's, past the enormous collection of perfume and cosmetic counters, and directly toward the blue neon JUNIORS sign. Wil took a sniff of the rose-scented air and watched as April immediately found the 40-percent-off rack and started pulling out dresses. "Ooh," she said, plucking out a pale blue strapless Nicole Miller and holding it up for Wil to see. "Isn't this gorgeous?"

Wil wrinkled her nose. "If you're going to prom." She ran her fingers across the soft, silky fabrics. "Seems a little too dressy for the Wellness Canyon end-of-summer party."

"You think?" April examined the dress and shrugged. "Well, it'll be fun to try on anyway."

Wil stepped away from the sale rack and fingered a sleek black Theory wrap dress with a thin lace trim along the deep neckline. Wil took it off the rack and held it up for April to see. "This would look nice on you."

April headed over to Wil, her arms full of dresses. "It's gorgeous," she said, tilting her head and looking at the dress Wil was holding. "But I look washed out in black. You should try it on, though." She circled the rack, her eyes peeled for the perfect addition to her load.

"What? *I'm* not going to the dance."

April looked up at Wil. "What do you mean? Of course you are!" Her eyes widened with worry. "Why else did you want to come to the mall?"

Wil shook her curly head. "Whatever. I'll try it on." Looking at the tag on the dress, Wil felt an uncharacteristic wave of apprehension. No way was she going to fit into any of the "normal" sizes they had here. But she thought she could at least amuse April.

Ten minutes later, Wil and April went into the dressing rooms, Wil with the black Theory dress and a chocolate brown empire-waist Nicole Miller and April with about twelve brightly colored and patterned dresses. Wil stepped into an empty, closet-sized dressing room and closed the door.

"Hey, April?" Wil started, pulling the Theory dress over her head and tugging it down. She waited to hear the awful sound of expensive fabric tearing apart because it couldn't fit over her body. But the sound never came. "Can I ask you something?"

"What's up?" April answered from the next dressing room.

"Was Colin your first kiss?" Wil asked tentatively as she shook the dress into place. She liked the way the silky fabric felt against her skin.

"Yeah," April called over the dressing room barrier. "Why?"

Wil laughed softly. "Me too," she told April. "Sucks that it was Colin, doesn't it? Aren't you supposed to remember them forever?" Wil slowly turned toward the mirror and looked at herself. She gasped, shocked, when she looked back and saw an almost-thin, relatively pretty girl looking back at her.

"Wil?" April's voice came from the next fitting room. "Can you zip me up?"

Wil stepped out, hoping there was no one else around

to see her. April was standing there in a bright fuchsia Betsey Johnson tank dress, one arm bent behind her to hold the dress together. Her face lit up when she saw Wil. "Ohmigod, you look awesome! Turn around!"

"Uh, no thanks," Wil said roughly, embarrassed. "Do you want me to zip you up or not?" April turned around obediently and let Wil zip her in. She immediately pranced over to the three-way mirror and spun around.

"That's a cool dress," Wil admitted reluctantly, looking at the way the shimmery material clung to her roommate's surprisingly toned body. She didn't want it to go to April's head, but she did look really pretty.

"Isn't it?" April said wistfully. "It just fits so much nicer than the others—and I love the color." She frowned, and in the three-way mirror, Wil could see three different versions of April's sad face. "But it's not one of the sale ones, so I definitely can't get it."

"Don't worry about it," Wil started, watching the way April lovingly touched the sides of the dress. Melanie's words came back to her and Wil imagined what it would be like to have to actually spend your own money. "I'll get it for you."

April spun around. "What? You can't do that."

"Really, I want to," Wil said, shrugging. Wil watched as April looked at herself in the mirror again and saw how much her heart was set on the dress. "Um . . . April? I don't really know how to tell you—Melanie told me that you paid for Wellness Canyon all on your own. I thought I should just let you know—that I know, I mean." Wil said in a rush.

April's face turned bright pink. "Oh," she whispered.

Wil hoped that April would accept the dress as a peace offering, as her way of saying she was sorry. "Besides, my parents would love it if they knew I was buying new clothes—even if they aren't exactly for me."

"Are you sure?" April asked, still a little incredulous. "I can pay you back."

"Not a chance." Wil grinned, thinking that maybe shopping could be a little fun after all. Maybe all it took was a friend to do it with.

# CHAPTER 31

**DATE:** August 8th

**FOOD:** 1 bowl of vegetable soup with whole-wheat pasta and water with lemon

**EXERCISE:** 30 sit-ups and 18 push-ups. I'm really trying to get my numbers up before the Olympics.

THE AFTERNOON RAIN THAT HAD SHROUDED WELLNESS CANYON in a light, almost-soothing mist the day before the Olympics had turned to a downpour after dinner. It pelted campers as they ran to the Lodge for free time. April stared out from under her plastic poncho at the lawn, waiting for Wil to give the signal that the coast was clear. As the last of the campers disappeared down the pathway, April patted the Ziploc bag full of crushed laxatives that was hidden under her poncho.

"Okay," Wil said, rain pooling in the brim of the black Burberry hat she'd impulsively bought when the girls were in the Macy's accessories department. Her blue eyes flashed in the gray darkness. "If we run into anyone, we'll each go to the Lodge and regroup."

April nodded. As they made soggy footprints across the lawn, the sound of the rain hitting the poncho crackled in April's ears and the aroma of wet grass filled her nose. She'd surprised herself when she said yes to ditching camp for a trip to the mall, and once they got back, she felt so good about the dress that Wil had bought for her that she immediately agreed that *this* should be the time they snuck into Colin's room to mix the laxatives into his protein powder. The rain helped too because no one in their right mind, except for Wil and April, would be wandering around outside.

Two figures suddenly emerged from Colin's dorm and Wil and April froze. In the dark, it was hard to tell who was outside Rockefeller, but the two girls stood still as the shadowy figures lingered, finally heading toward the auditorium. Wil watched them disappear into the rain and then motioned for April to move forward.

Rockefeller was empty except for someone banging around in a room on the second floor. Unlike Franklin, Colin's building was more like a college dorm, with two common spaces on each floor. Wil and April had suffered through Colin's endless bragging about having a suite off the first floor common area, so when they approached the first room, they weren't surprised to see that the door was decorated like he and Gregg *were* actually living in a college dorm. A giant poster of the USC campus was taped to the outside along with a Yeah Yeah Yeahs bumper sticker.

Wil reached up and knocked on the door. They'd worked

out in advance that if Colin or Gregg actually answered, they'd tell them that Melanie had put them in charge of making sure everyone knew that the evening event—a concert by a local band—started right after dinner. They had even gone so far as to sow the seeds of doubt about the time with a few other campers in case they needed the story to bail them out.

"Gone," April said, looking down at the floor to see if they had left footprints, but the hallway runner had soaked up the rain from their shoes.

Wil tried the handle and the lock caught. She pulled the paper clip from her back pocket and worked the lock. She tried the handle again. Still locked.

"You said you could open it," April complained, choking back a mild panic in her throat.

"Chill," Wil hissed. She bent the paper clip and continued working, the lock clicking just as it had when Wil practiced on their own door. "Voila."

A breeze of cologne and some unidentified male smells hit them as the door swung open. Wil reached into her pocket and fished out the flashlight she'd purchased at the mall. April followed the beam of light as it roamed over piles of dirty clothes and a small stack of ESPN magazines near what April assumed was Colin's bed. On the small nightstand between the beds was Colin's green Nalgene bottle next to a canister of protein powder with a piece of masking tape that said MAGIC POWDER across the label.

"Sweet," Wil said under her breath. She shone the flashlight on the canister and April moved forward. "Go keep watch," Wil said, nodding toward the door.

"No," April whispered. "I want to do it." The assertiveness in her voice surprised her, and it must have surprised Wil too. But she handed the flashlight to April and moved to the door without a word.

April seemed to float through the room, pulling the Ziploc bag out of the pocket of her sagging Gap chinos that stayed up only because her belt was secured on the tightest notch. She grabbed the protein powder and popped the top on the canister, the room suddenly smelling like fake strawberries. She tilted it into the flashlight's beam and sighed in relief. Wil said she'd seen all kinds of protein powders over the years and some were brownish—in which case the laxative would stand out. But the protein powder was white, so the laxative was indistinguishable from it. April mixed the concoction together with the spoon they'd smuggled out of the dining hall. She replaced the lid and gave Wil a thumbs-up. Wil stepped back into the flashlight beam and April could see that she had a single box of laxatives in her hand.

"What's that?" April whispered hoarsely.

"Insurance," Wil said in her normal voice, which startled April. April watched as she tucked the box of laxatives deep into Colin's gym bag, burying them under a pile of clothes and Colin's sneakers, holding her nose between her thumb and forefinger. "This stuff reeks," Wil coughed out.

"Let's get out of here," April said, rushing for the door, her nerves tingling with delight at the prospect of getting even with Colin. Wil casually turned the lock on the back of the doorknob and pulled the door closed behind her. The girls gave each other a high five and giggled on their way back to the Lodge.

# CHAPTER 32

**DATE:** August 9th

**FOOD:** I large cup of coffee and a small egg-white omelet with I tbsp. goat cheese.

**EXERCISE:** I did a secret round of sit-ups while April was in the shower . . . but only to test myself for the Olympics.

NERVOUS EXCITEMENT PERMEATED THE DINING HALL THE MORNING of the Wellness Canyon Olympics. Even though Melanie, Kevin, and the other counselors encouraged everyone to eat a hearty meal, people only nibbled at their egg-white omelets, afraid of just throwing them up later.

"I woke up with a cramp in my leg," Paul admitted. Even *he* pushed away his breakfast only half eaten. "I just drank like two gallons of water to try to work it out." He stretched his leg under the table, rubbing his calf muscle.

"You probably just slept on it wrong," Dave told him, casually taking another sip of his fruit smoothie. "How're you, April?"

April tapped her fingers nervously against her tray of uneaten food. She smiled, though Wil could tell she was anxious. "Ready to win." She glanced at Wil and actually gave her a wink.

Wil watched as Colin greeted Gregg with a show-offy high five at the breakfast bar. Colin was gripping his Nalgene full of protein powder as usual, and Wil exchanged looks with April, who smiled when Wil looked at her. They both watched as Colin dumped the powder into one of the blenders and topped it off with strawberries and orange slices. Jessica snuck up behind him and slapped his butt as the blender whirred. Colin pretended to be angry but then cracked a smile when Jessica patted his arm.

Colin poured his protein shake back into his Nalgene, dropping the blender pitcher into a plastic bin of dirty dishes. Wil held her breath as Colin slugged back half the protein shake. She examined his face, worrying that he'd spit it back up, but he drank the rest of the shake down. She and April punched knuckles lightly under the table and continued to watch Colin as he took a seat at Jessica and Marci's table.

Wil shielded her eyes from the sun and tried not to worry. The back of the laxative boxes said it would take an hour or so to kick in, but she secretly hoped it would work right away.

"Anything yet?" April asked quietly as the girls got up and followed Paul and Dave out to the lawn.

"Nada," Wil answered, bending down to retie her shoes. She wanted to make sure she was prepared—for everything.

"Okay, I hope you're ready!" Melanie called out through a

megaphone from the Lodge porch. "Can I have the counselors up here for a minute, please, before we start?"

Kevin and the rest of the counselors gathered around Melanie while the campers moved restlessly down on the lawn, getting ready for the first event. Everyone was stretching, stomping their feet, tying their shoelaces, and generally trying not to look nervous. The day was already hot and the sun had luckily dried up the lawn from the rainfall the night before.

Wil, April, Dave, and Paul stood in a circle as the counselors broke apart and fanned out across the lawn, taking their various stations. Each had a silver stopwatch hanging around their neck and a clipboard to record the results.

For the first event, the relay race, Melanie pitted two teams against each other, with two members of each team on opposite sides of the lawn. "This challenge will test your team's communication skills and it is also designed so that you can see how difficult it is to maneuver with extra weight," she said, holding up a set of wrist and ankle weights. "You'll run across the lawn wearing these and then, at the other end, you'll undo them and pass them to your teammate, who will then put them on, run back, and pass them off to the next one, and so on. You must be wearing them and they must be completely fastened before you start your turn. Otherwise, you will get a time penalty, or even be disqualified. Runners, ready?" Melanie didn't wait for an answer and instead blew her whistle, officially inaugurating the annual Wellness Canyon Olympics. The first heat took off, the all-girls team taking the lead. The remaining campers clapped and cheered as the second heat began to line up.

"Next two teams," Melanie called out as Kevin and Cammie conferred with her about the results. Wil stepped forward, Marci on the other side of her. Paul and Gregg were behind them, respectively, and April was across the lawn with Dave, avoiding Colin, who was jogging in place. Melanie handed Wil the weights and Wil fastened them around her wrists and ankles. "Wait for the whistle," Melanie instructed, moving off to the side.

The whistle chirped and Wil pushed off, pumping her arms to propel herself in front of Marci. Both girls struggled against the extra weight and fought for the lead. Wil had seen a previous camper try to cheat the system by only doing up the ankle weights halfway, but one had fallen off mid-stride, costing her team a dozen or more added seconds to their time. Wil pounded across the lawn in no time, rapidly approaching April. April planted her feet, getting ready to help Wil rip the weights off. Suddenly, Marci shrieked as she undid the Velcro on her weights and passed them to Jessica. Wil hurried to put the weights into April's hands and April put them on and sped off, matching Jessica before handing off the weights to Paul, whose cramp had clearly worked itself out as he and Gregg ran side by side toward Dave and Colin.

Paul slid in next to Dave and tore off his weights. He stuck them out in front of him, almost ramming them into Dave's chest, which made Dave flinch before he grabbed the weights, put them on, and turned to run the final distance. Colin was a good three steps in front of Dave, and Wil watched as the gap widened. Wil crossed her fingers, praying the laxatives would take effect, crippling Colin before he could cross the finish line.

But Colin breezed across the line and kept going, slowing and turning a wide arc around the other campers, who were clapping and cheering for him. Colin handed the weights to Kevin so that he could do a little victory dance as Dave crossed the finish line, dropped the weight, and doubled over, his hands on his knees.

Wil put her hands on her hips and turned to April, lowering her voice. "Are you sure you did it right?"

"Yes, I'm *sure*," April said again, getting annoyed.

"You mixed it up good?" Wil asked, making a mixing gesture with her hand.

"For the tenth time, yes!" April smoothed her hair behind her ear.

"Just asking." Wil held her up her hands. Wil wanted to get back at Colin, sure, and the fact that camp was officially over the next morning meant they'd lose any further chance at revenge. But also, their team was in *second* place. Eight weeks ago a silver medal wouldn't have mattered at all to Wil, but being so close to the gold had kick-started her appetite to win. A silver medal was as good as coming in last if it meant that Colin's team was going to win.

# CHAPTER 33

**DATE:** August 9th

**FOOD:** Low-fat chicken salad in a whole-wheat pita with lettuce and tomato. Oh, and a banana and a fat-free yogurt—I need to keep up my energy!

**EXERCISE:** That relay race was freaking hard!

That afternoon, the campers lined up on the lawn for the second round of events. After the relay race that morning, everyone had participated in a swimming race, which Jessica had won for Colin's team. Then, they'd all gathered back on the lawn for the Wellness Canyon trivia contest, where April had totally beaten out the competition. It seemed that all her time reading the brochures before coming to camp had finally paid off.

"Okay, guys!" Kevin said, spreading his arms wide as if trying to fit all of the camp into them. "Time for the sit-ups contest. Cammie and I will lead you through this one, so come on!"

Everyone got up slowly and moved over under the large oak tree on the lawn where there was, thankfully, quite a bit of shade.

Kevin continued explaining the challenge. "Similar to the fitness tests way back at the beginning of the summer, you will pair with your roommate for help. You'll each do as many sit-ups as you can within two minutes and then you'll switch. Your number will be added together with those of your other teammates and that result will determine our winner. So everyone get into place!"

Half of the campers lay down on the lawn, ready to begin. Their roommates all sat at their feet, ready to count. April got into position on the dry grass and put her arms behind her head. Wil tightened her grip around April's ankles and nodded, a serious look on her flushed face.

"Ready?" Kevin called out, looking at his stopwatch. "Go!"

The campers struggled through the event, only stopping for the quick switch of partners. April sweated through three dozen sit-ups in the afternoon heat. Wil did about twenty, and Paul and Dave had performed a whopping sixty each. Unfortunately, Colin did over one hundred sit-ups just on his own, so his team was impossible to beat. The counselors let the campers rest on the lawn for a few minutes to recuperate before the last half of the events: the tape measure toss, the shoe kick, and the climbing wall.

April and her teammates huddled in a circle and stretched their sore muscles.

"We're gonna lose at this rate," Dave said, kicking the ground with the toe of his New Balance sneaker.

"Guys, come on!" April encouraged, bouncing up and down on the balls of her feet to stretch out her calves. "We won the trivia and came in second in just about everything else. We still have a chance!" she said, even though she knew they had some serious ground to cover if they ever wanted to catch up.

"Yeah, but we'd have to win *everything* else to do that. There's just no way," Paul moaned, shrugging. April knew he was probably right, but she wished that her teammates were a little more optimistic.

"Okay, campers!" Melanie's voice broke through the chatter on the lawn. "It's time for the tape measure toss! Everyone come over to me!" The campers all walked over to the far end of the lawn where Melanie was standing.

"Each team will be designated a colored tape measure," Melanie continued, holding up a small orange disc, roughly the size of a hockey puck. "One by one, you and your teammates will come up here and toss the tape measure—that's under-handed, please—in this direction." She pointed over toward where Kevin and some of the other counselors were standing by a large tree. "They have colored flags that correspond to your tape measures. When all of you have tossed your tape measures, they will place a flag in the ground where it landed. Whichever team tosses the farthest wins. Everyone understand?"

Some murmurs sounded through the crowd, and April surveyed the area. She didn't have a great arm, but she had always been surprisingly good at things like horseshoes and bowling.

"Okay, first team up is Colin, Gregg, Jessica, and Marci!"

Everyone cheered as the team lined up by Melanie. Gregg stepped forward and Melanie handed him a small orange tape measure. "Good luck!" she said.

Gregg leaned back and looked at the expanse of grass in front of him. Then he took a step forward and swung his arm like he was throwing a shot put. The tape measure flew in the air and landed *really* far away, making his whole team cheer. "Oh yeah," Gregg said, walking back to join his team as Kevin pranced after it and put an orange flag in the ground. He brought the tape measure back to Melanie, and Jessica stepped forward to take her turn.

"Come on, Jessie! You can do it!" Marci yelled, jumping up and down. She grabbed Gregg's hand as she cheered.

Jessica looked like she was concentrating very hard as she tossed the tape measure. It kind of flopped when it hit the ground just a few feet away, and she giggled. "Oh well!" she said, giving Marci a high five, anyway. April heard Colin groan.

Marci went next and threw her tape measure a little farther than Jessica, but still nowhere near Gregg's. She walked back to her group looking a little disappointed.

Last, Colin stepped forward and took his place at the starting line. He grabbed the tape measure from Melanie and swung his arm forward with a flourish. Clearly, he'd thought that his powerful toss would make the tape measure go farther than it did, but instead it went high, high, high in the air until it landed about ten feet behind Gregg's orange flag. "Crap!" Colin exclaimed.

"Colin! Language!" Melanie reprimanded while Kevin put a flag in the ground where Colin's toss had landed. Then she called the next team forward to toss their blue tape measures.

April's team watched anxiously through thirteen more rounds before they were finally called. Everyone had done fairly well, but Colin's team was still in the lead from Gregg's triumphant throw.

"And last we have April, Wil, Paul, and Dave!" Melanie called out to the campers. Everyone clapped as the team stepped forward and April took her place at the front, ready to throw. Melanie handed April the pink tape measure and winked as she took it.

"Come on, April!" Wil shouted from behind her.

"Yeah, April!" Dave added in. "You can do it!"

Bolstered by her teammates' encouragement, April took a step forward and tossed the tape measure as far as she could. She held her breath as she watched it soar through the air until it landed a few feet shy of Gregg's. *Yes!* She grinned as she walked back to join her teammates.

"That was amazing, April," Dave told her, grabbing her hand. "I hope the rest of us can keep up."

"Me too!" April enthused, giving his slightly sweaty hand a friendly squeeze.

Then Wil stepped forward and took her turn. April watched her throw it with all her might, and the measure landed about ten feet shy of April's. "All right, Wil!" April yelled, jumping up and down.

Next, Paul stepped forward and threw. The tape measure landed between April's and Gregg's. Close, but still not bringing their team into the lead. The campers cheered and April saw Colin and Gregg give each other a high five, thinking themselves a shoo-in for the win.

Finally, Dave stepped forward and took his spot next to Melanie. She handed him the tape measure and smiled. "Okay everyone!" Melanie said, not letting Dave start right away. "If Dave gets this shot, he'll win it for their team. If not, then Gregg wins the challenge!" Melanie clearly wanted to add some suspense and it worked. Everyone moved in a little closer and began cheering louder for the last throw.

Dave appeared to whisper something to the tape measure and looked straight ahead toward Gregg's orange flag. He took a couple of practice swings and then flung the tape measure hard. The pink plastic disk soared through the air and landed right next to Gregg's flag. Everyone struggled to see who had actually won and Kevin ran forward to make the final call. He picked up the tape measure and jammed a pink flag into the ground—just inches beyond Gregg's.

"And Dave is the winner!" Melanie called, entering the results into her BlackBerry. "Congratulations!"

Dave, Paul, Wil, and April jumped up and down in a huddle, laughing. April looked at her roommate and grinned. Even if the laxatives didn't end up working on Colin, their team still had a chance to kick his butt. And April knew *that* was what was important.

# CHAPTER 34

**DATE:** August 9th
**FOOD:** 1 Lemon Zest Luna bar.
**EXERCISE:** The Olympics!

APRIL AND HER TEAMMATES GATHERED TOWARD THE FAR END OF the lawn with the rest of campers. They'd been scheduled last for the climbing wall, against Colin's team, because they were currently neck and neck: Colin's team had won the weight relay, the swimming race, and the sit-up challenge. April's team had won the tape measure toss, the Wellness Canyon trivia contest, and, surprisingly, the shoe kick. Now it all came down to the climbing competition.

During lunch, the campers had watched curiously as a crowd of men in matching green-and-white T-shirts had quickly assembled a climbing wall under Melanie's watchful gaze. Now that it had been secured on the lawn, the wall loomed ominously over the grass, casting long shadows in the mid-afternoon light. The campers had hoped the final challenge would take place at Huge Rock, but the counselors said the secured wall was safer.

"Oh! They have one of these at my school," Paul said confidently. "No problem."

April looked at him skeptically. "Yeah, but it's for time, remember," she said. "Not just making it to the top."

"If you just keep your footing on the little fake rocks, you're fine," Paul said.

"And you get to wear those harnesses," Dave said, pointing at the swinglike devices hanging at the ends of the ropes from the top of the wall. "So even if you fall, you just kind of hang in the air."

"But what if you're afraid of heights?" Wil asked, eyeing the top of the wall.

April glanced at her. "Are you?"

"No." Wil shrugged. "Just wondering."

"Well, it's not that high anyway," Dave added.

Everyone watched in anticipation as the first two teams scaled the wall, one player from each team strapped into a harness at a time. Some campers were slower than others, taking whole minutes to get to the top. April looked across the lawn, a little envious of all the other campers who already knew they hadn't won—girls lying in the grass, braiding flowers into each other's hair as they waited to see the results, only interested in watching.

Colin stashed his Propel Fitness Water in his gym bag and dropped to the lawn for a round of push-ups as his team moved closer to competition.

Wil leaned closer to April. "Why aren't they working?"

"Shhh. I don't know," April said, frantically looking around to see if anyone could hear them. The teams were so close and April wanted to win so badly. But not as badly as she wanted to get back at Colin. She didn't know what could have gone wrong.

Suddenly, Melanie called April's name, pairing her up against Jessica, and April's stomach felt like she'd hoped Colin's would. "Good luck," Jessica said, smiling at April as they strapped themselves into the harnesses.

"Thanks." She smiled back at Jessica. "You too." April double-checked her harness and looked up at the wall, willing herself to think only of beating Colin.

"Ready," Melanie called. The girls looked at each other and wiggled around, each trying to get the best footing. "Go!" The girls took off up the wall, April concentrating fiercely on each little foothold as she rose higher than Jessica.

"Go!" Wil screamed.

"You can do it!" Dave screamed louder.

The cheers were like a strong wind at April's back and her limbs felt light as wings as she scaled the wall. She forced herself not to look back as Jessica yelled out something about jamming her thumb.

"You're almost there!" Dave yelled, his voice cracking.

April reached for the last rock and pulled herself up to the top. A round of applause went up, but April didn't dare look down. She backed down the wall easily, focusing on the sky and letting gravity doing most of the work.

As April crawled out of the harness, Jessica worked her way back to the bottom. "Nice climb." Jessica smiled. She stuck out her hand and April shook it.

"Thanks," April said. She smiled back at Jessica as Kevin helped her out of her harness.

Wil moved forward next, grabbing the harness from April and putting it on. "Awesome job!" Wil said genuinely as she high-fived April and took her position at the wall.

"Good luck," Marci said as they both strapped in.

"Luck has nothing to do with it," Wil said.

April, Paul, and Dave looked on in amazement as Wil scampered easily up the climbing wall. She seemed to float about the foot and handholds, beating Marci handily.

"Yes!" Wil pumped her fist as Melanie called out her time, the best of the day. "That's how it's done, ladies and gentlemen." Wil took a bow while Marci still struggled to get out of the harness.

Wil sauntered back over to her teammates looking elated.

"How the hell did you do that?" Dave asked Wil, shaking his head in wonder.

"Hey, I'm up," Paul said sheepishly. He slapped his hands against his cheeks, as if to wake himself up.

"Go get 'em, man," Dave said.

Paul shrugged and struggled his way into the harness. At Melanie's call, he and Gregg started up the wall. Gregg practically left Paul behind in a cloud of dust and April had to look away.

"C'mon," Wil said in disgust. "Get your butt up there!"

Melanie shot Wil a look. "Hey! None of that."

Wil forced a smile onto her face. "You can do it, Paul!" Wil and April looked at each other, each knowing that Paul had absolutely no chance of beating Gregg up the wall.

Gregg easily beat Paul up and back. His hands slipped from the handholds several times and Kevin and Melanie surrounded him for the final distance in case he slipped and fell.

"It's okay, Paul," April said. "It was a good try." Paul just shook his head, not able to meet anyone's eyes. Wil patted his sweaty back.

Melanie recalculated the times while Dave and Colin stood in front of the climbing wall, waiting for their turn. "It's a perfect tie," she announced, looking up from her BlackBerry. "Whoever wins this wins the Olympics!" The crowd of campers let out a whoop of excitement and April turned around, noticing that several people who were disinterested before had come back over to watch the last heated match of the summer.

"I should warn you," Colin announced as he parted the crowd. He stretched his arms out in front of him. "I'm part mountain man."

"Oh, that's what stinks!" Wil said loudly. Colin shot her a look as everyone laughed.

"All right, go time," Dave said, strapping into the harness. He caught April's eye across the crowd.

"You got it, Dave," April shouted, but she knew it was hopeless. Dave easily had thirty pounds on Colin and much less discernible muscle. It would take a miracle. The crowd tightened around the climbing wall as Melanie checked Colin and Dave's harnesses. Marci and Jessica, in their matching short red running shorts, were bouncing up and down with excitement.

"Good luck, lard-o." Colin winked at Dave.

"Yeah, good luck," Dave said tentatively, looking up at the wall.

Suddenly, Colin groaned, rubbing his stomach. April grabbed Wil's hand and squeezed. Wil smiled at April as Colin made a squinty face.

"Ready?" Melanie called out. The crowd became silent.

Colin nodded, as if the question had just been directed at him.

The sound of the whistle blared across the lawn and Dave and Colin mounted the climbing wall. Dave moved froglike up the wall, scrambling a full body length in front of Colin.

"Go, Colin!" Jessica yelled, egging him on, her blond ponytail bobbing. Colin raised his leg to catch one of the footholds and an audible fart escaped. A few people in the front row exchanged glances and started to snicker. April and Wil traded smiles as Colin looked over his shoulder to see if anyone had noticed. He climbed another foot and a sound like a clap of thunder filled the air. Jessica covered her mouth in embarrassment as Marci laughed. April watched in delight as Dave moved way ahead of Colin, who had stopped.

"Oh yeah," Wil said under her breath, clenching her hands in fists to keep from laughing. "Here it comes."

Colin clung to the wall and let out another sonorous fart, a sheen of sweat covering his face. Then, as he tried to reach up for the next handhold, an extremely loud, foul-smelling fart escaped from him and his eyes went wide with shock. Colin reached back to shield his shorts from view and lost his balance, falling off the wall. He plummeted to the ground, the harness snapping tight just as his butt was about to smash into the ground.

"Ewww!" The campers nearest the wall took two steps back. Jessica, Marci, and Gregg scattered along with the others. Colin stumbled to his feet, covering his face as he pushed through the crowd.

"Colin! Colin, where are you going?" Melanie screeched after him, a confused look on her face.

"Bathroom!" Colin yelled back, running with his hand on his butt the whole way. All the campers tittered and whispered as he ran.

Dave slowly cruised down the climbing wall. "Hey! I won! Hello?" He tried to get his teammates' attention to celebrate his victory, but everyone was focused on Colin.

Wil and April shared another smile and April's heart soared. She wondered if Colin had *ever* been that humiliated in his whole pathetic life.

# CHAPTER 35

**DATE:** August 9th
**FOOD:** Who cares?!
**EXERCISE:** Winning the Olympics!!

"AND IN FIRST PLACE AT THE WELLNESS CANYON OLYMPICS ARE . . . Dave, Paul, April, and Wil! Congratulations!" Kevin screeched, pointing at Wil's team. "Come on up, guys!"

Dave rushed the wooden platform that had been constructed for the awards ceremony. Melanie darted around and placed a beautiful golden Wellness Canyon medal around each of the teammates' necks. Wil ducked under the purple ribbon, the medal falling heavy against her chest. The others did the same and the four contestants raised their arms triumphantly above their heads, basking in the glow of the applause from the rest of the campers.

Wil looked out over the campers and saw Colin, who had apparently snuck back to the group after changing his shorts. He looked a little embarrassed and was totally ignoring everything happening around him. For a split second, Wil felt a little guilty. If she and April hadn't put the laxatives in Colin's drink, then their team would never have won in the first place. But then she looked around at her teammates just as Dave gave April a giant bear hug, picking her up off her feet and swinging her around in a circle as she giggled uncontrollably.

"Yes!" Paul bounced his head like a boxer making his way to the ring.

Wil pumped her fist in the air and she and April exchanged high fives while the other campers whistled and hollered. They were *way* too happy for Wil to feel upset about anything. Besides, Colin would be fine—in another couple of years he would be playing for USC. Wil, April, Dave, and Paul would be lucky if they ever won anything again. The crowd cheered again as Kevin called up the silver medalists, an all-girl team. Wil clapped for the girls, genuinely happy for them.

Wil watched as Colin reached into his bag and rummaged around. He yanked his gray hoodie down and sent a box of laxatives flying . . . directly at Melanie's feet.

Suddenly everything and everybody stopped. It was like some cheesy movie where someone says or does something horrible and the party music stops playing. Everyone stared at the box in silence and then started pointing and whispering.

"Quiet!" Melanie yelled out, a furious look on her face. "Colin! My office. Now."

Wil nudged April and looked at her out of the corner of her eye. They both smiled as they watched Melanie lead Colin away.

# CHAPTER 36

**DATE:** August 9th

**FOOD:** I just had some Diet Coke and a spinach salad for dinner. I was so afraid my dress wouldn't fit!

**EXERCISE:** A quick cardio session on the elliptical this afternoon. See above.

APRIL STARED INTO THE FULL-LENGTH MIRROR AT THE FOOT OF HER bed and smoothed her hands over her dress. A summer of shorts and T-shirts had obscured her body, and while she knew that she'd lost weight, she was surprised at how the dress revealed an almost entirely new body. It was suddenly real: this was her. April twisted in front of the mirror, admiring the fruits of her labor. She'd gone away for the summer and was about to come back home, a completely new and improved person. She was already imagining the look on Olivia St. James's face as she scooted over to make room for April at her lunch table.

April unzipped her shiny pink makeup bag and pulled out a tiny container of Stila eye shadow. As she swiped the shimmering soft pink shadow across her eyelids, she could see

Wil, sprawled out on her bed. She had one iPod earbud in and her nose stuck in *The Perks of Being a Wallflower*, the latest novel from the huge stack that had sat at the foot of her bed all summer, and she was nonchalantly doing some leg raises at the same time.

"I still can't believe he's confined to his room tonight," April said, trying to hide how happy she actually was about Colin's punishment. April twisted the cap off her Maybelline Great Lash mascara and carefully brushed it onto her short, pale eyelashes. She blinked and examined her eyes, hoping she hadn't overdone it.

"Serves him right." Wil grinned and looked up from her book.

April dropped the mascara back into her bag and searched for the right lipstick. Maybe just a gloss? She didn't want to look like she was trying too hard. She was a little sad—only a little— that Colin wasn't going to be there to see how awesome she looked. She had envisioned him asking her to dance and just laughing in his face. April turned around suddenly and glanced at Wil's silver alarm clock. "You'd better start getting ready."

"Mmmm...I don't think so." Wil waved her book at April. "I'm almost done with this, and I really want to finish it before I go home."

"What?" April put her hands on her hips. "You've got to come! I don't want to go alone! Besides, you bought that dress!"

"Oh, it doesn't matter. My parents won't care. Besides,

dances aren't really my thing." Wil shook her head and smiled wryly. "But I don't think you'll be alone." She closed her book on her finger. "You look too pretty for that."

April was shocked to hear a compliment like that come out of Wil's lips. It was so . . . *nice.* "You sure you won't come?" April glanced at herself in the mirror once again. The idea of going without Wil made her a little sad.

"I'm sure." Wil tossed the book to the end of her bed and pulled out her earbud. "But hey—meet me up at Huge Rock afterward, at like eleven thirty." She raised and lowered her eyebrows mysteriously. "I've got a little something planned."

"What is it?" April asked, curious. She loved surprises.

"Guess you'll just have to show up and find out." A knock at the door caused them both to jump. Wil bounced off her bed and opened the door.

"It must be for you," Wil said in a singsong voice, revealing Dave, standing in the doorway in a black sports jacket, tie, and brand-new jeans. April had to do a double take; she barely recognized him. "Nice threads." Wil touched the sleeve of Dave's jacket and then looked down at his jeans "Are those Diesel?"

"Yeah, I think so." Dave replied, tugging at the tie knot to try to loosen it from around his neck. "My parents gave them to me at the beginning of the summer as an incentive—like it would inspire me to work hard so I could fit into them."

April blushed momentarily, thinking of her own Habitual jeans she'd bought exactly for that purpose. "Well, it looks like it worked." She turned to the mirror to cover her embarrassment and applied some Burt's Bees strawberry lip gloss across her lips. She took one last look at herself and was pleased. She had used Wil's hair straightener to make her hair look sleeker, like Jessica's. And combined with the shimmery dress that was a size smaller than she ever thought possible, she actually *felt* pretty.

"I thought maybe I could walk you to the dance," Dave said, looking directly at April. He ran his hand through his gelled hair and then nervously wiped it on his pants. "Are you ready?" His voice was tentative and shy.

April blushed again and smoothed her hair behind her ears. She appraised herself in the mirror one more time and then breathed deeply. "Okay, I'm all set." And she was. She had never been more ready in her life.

"Have fun, you two!" Wil waved goodbye as April and Dave headed out the door.

The heels of April's silver peep-toed sandals sank into the grass as soon as she stepped onto the lawn, and Dave gently held her arm for balance as she took them off and shuffled through the cool grass barefoot. The entire lawn was lit by the full moon.

"You look really hot," Dave said, looking at April from the corner of his eye. She looked up at him as he winced. "I mean, you look great."

"Thanks," April said, aware of the sway of her hips for the first time that she could remember. She pinched the inside of her newly trim bicep to make sure it wasn't all a dream. Just the thought of waking up and being the old April again made her queasy. Thankfully, the pinch hurt. This was real.

They crossed the rest of the lawn in silence, headed toward the sound of thumping music in the distance. Other campers in cute dresses, button-down shirts, and blazers approached Dickinson, which had been transformed into a nightclub. As they stepped inside the wide-open doors, they were stunned by the number of colored lights and streamers draping the room. A silver banner reading CONGRATULATIONS! YOU DID IT! in shiny red letters hung across the far wall over the long buffet tables full of gorgeous—but healthy, of course—snacks and hors d'oeuvres. Smaller, circular tables were spread around the edges of the dance floor, already peppered with barefoot girls in dresses. A giant mirrored disco ball hung in the center of the dance floor, sending shimmering shards of light across the room.

Dave whistled, straightening his tie again as his eyes took in the scene. "Is there a bar?"

April laughed nervously. Her self-doubt returned with full force the second she saw the room full of happy, chatting people. Paul spotted them from next to the punch bowl and worked his way over, a glass in each hand. "Actually pretty nice, huh?" He drained a glass of punch and then slipped the full glass into the empty one. "But at least be glad you missed the Michael Jackson." Paul smiled and began to do a little move that looked vaguely like the moonwalk.

Gregg crossed the dance floor and April felt a lump in her throat. A wave of panic overtook her. What if Gregg confronted her about framing Colin? She watched Gregg fill a plastic cup with punch and prayed he wouldn't move in her direction.

"Let's grab a table," April said, wiping her palms against the sides of her dress.

"I got one in the corner." Paul nodded toward it, leading the way.

The three sat around the table and April was immediately sad. She sat at tables in the corner *before* she looked fabulous, and now that she *was* more like the popular girls she had always dreamed of becoming, she didn't want to be stuck in the corner. Paul and Dave started up a conversation about the Matrix movies that they'd clearly started somewhere before—maybe they'd been arguing about them the entire summer—and April looked around to see if anyone might be listening. She scanned the crowd, admiring all the campers in their nice dresses and button-downs. A steady beat of synthesizer came through the speakers and Dave immediately looked up. "This is my favorite song," he said, snapping his fingers. He looked at April. "Would you . . . Do you want to dance?"

"Yeah, okay." April nodded. At least she could get out of the corner. The song, something April didn't quite recognize but knew she'd heard before, wasn't only Dave's favorite song: *everyone* seemed to mob the dance floor. April felt the music surge through her and she swayed, her hair brushing from shoulder to shoulder. Some of the other guys just shuffled their feet to the music or lip-synced the lyrics into imaginary microphones. She hadn't guessed that Dave would know how to dance, but he held his own.

In the middle of the dance floor, she spotted Jessica and Marci, Jessica in a black satin minidress that made her look absolutely tiny and Marci in some kind of wine-colored monstrosity that looked she'd wrapped some drapes around her. Jessica looked up suddenly and caught April's eye. April was about to look away when Jessica waved at her, her silver bangle bracelets glittering in the disco ball light. April smiled and waved back. The chorus repeated and Dave spun April around and around, smiling at her whenever their eyes met.

The song ended and April smiled at Dave. "Thanks," Dave said breathlessly, wiping tiny beads of sweat off his forehead. "They could play that one again. Everyone loved it." He looked around as the dance floor emptied.

"I'm going to get something to drink," April said, watching as Jessica and Marci headed toward the snack table.

"I'll get it for you," Dave offered, fingering the buttons on his shirt.

"It's okay. I'll be right back." April turned and headed for the punch bowl.

Jessica was ladling a cup of punch for Marci, who took it and spit her gum into a napkin. Jessica's eyelids were covered with a gold, glittery eye shadow.

"Could you pass me a cup?" April asked, smiling politely at Jessica and Marci.

"Sure," Jessica replied, not really looking up. Then she handed April a cup. "Ooh, that dress is amazing," Jessica exclaimed appreciatively.

April blushed. "Oh, thanks. Um . . . I love yours, too." She took a sip of punch.

"You must have lost, like, fifty pounds!" Jessica grabbed April's hand and spun her around, smiling at her appreciatively.

"Finally able to ditch your loser roommate?" Marci asked, smiling as she sidled up to Jessica and April, popping a cube of cheese into her mouth.

April started to defend Wil and then stopped, remembering how she had felt about Jessica and Marci at the beginning of the summer—and how she had felt about Wil. And then Marci moved closer to April and continued, "You know, Wil was in my share group this summer."

"Oh yeah, Marce, tell her the story." Jessica stepped a little closer and her gold-shadowed eyes got really wide.

"So we were in our share group on the first day and Wil said that you were really annoying and that you were only here because you were trying to fit into a stupid pair of jeans that you brought with you," Marci explained, taking a sip of her punch. Even though April knew that the comment was from so early in the summer—and that she had despised Wil just as much—it still felt like a huge punch in the stomach.

"But *we* knew that wasn't true," Jessica put in quickly, looking at Marci pointedly.

"Oh yeah, totally. I mean, we even saw how obnoxious she was at orientation. I can't believe you got stuck with such an awful team this summer!" Marci said, her face positively dripping with pity. April didn't know what to say or even think, so she just smiled tightly and took a sip of her punch. Wil's words—no matter how old—reminded April of just how awful the first half of the summer was. She was suddenly really glad to be at the dance with Marci and Jessica.

Suddenly, Gregg appeared, wrapping his arms around Marci's now unquestionably thin waist. "What's happening, ladies?" He refilled his glass and looked around before pulling a tiny bottle of vodka from his pocket and pouring it into his punch.

"You have to know everything about us, don't you?" Jessica kidded, making a pouty face with her glossy red lips.

*Us?* Was Jessica finally including her in that *us?* It sounded good, even if it was a little late—they were all going home tomorrow, after all.

"Hey, congrats on the gold," Gregg said, turning to April. His dark eyes looked her up and down, and even though he wasn't gorgeous or anything, it was still nice to be looked at like that.

"Yeah," Jessica said, smoothing her hair behind her ears. "I mean, we were bummed, but your team *totally* deserved to win."

April took a gulp of her punch and tried to smile brightly, though inside she was still seething about Wil. "Thanks."

Marci nudged Gregg, and he poured some of his vodka into Marci's cup. "I still laugh my ass off every time I think of Colin at the climbing wall," Marci said as Gregg finished pouring.

"Yeah, that was crazy. What exactly happened to him?" April asked the question without thinking and then suddenly worried that they all knew she had something to do with it.

"Laxatives." Marci shook her head, wisps of short reddish brown hair slipping out of her rhinestone barrettes. "It's *so* lame. I'm glad he's not here." She took a big sip of her punch, leaving a purplish lipstick stain on the rim of the cup.

"Anyway, you should totally come hang out with us," Jessica said, elbowing April in the side. "I know it's the last night and all, but better late than never, right?"

"Yeah, *totally.*" Marci blinked her extra-long lashes at April. "I hardly talked to anyone this entire summer. Weird, right?"

"You know . . ." Jessica started, looking down at her red-painted toenails, sticking out of her strappy sandals. "We, uh . . . we should've said something that day in the dining hall." Jessica looked up at April, her baby blue eyes wide and sincere. "I don't know why we let Colin embarrass you like that." She bit her lip, leaving a tiny red stain on her front teeth. "I'm really sorry."

"Yeah, me too," Marci piped up. "Colin was always doing stuff like that." April definitely remembered Marci laughing at her, along with Colin, as she walked out of the dining hall that day that felt like forever ago. But it didn't matter anymore—they were actually apologizing about it.

"Oh, it's okay," April said, waving her hand like it was

no big deal, which it suddenly wasn't. Yeah, it had hurt, but so many different people had hurt her, and at least Jessica and Marci were kind and honest—it was more than she could get from her own roommate. "I've totally forgotten about it."

"Hey," Jessica started, smiling at April sweetly. "Where's your date?"

April nearly spit out her punch. "Oh, he's *not* my date," April shouted over the loud beat of a new song.

"Oh my God!" Jessica's eyes flew open wide. "It's *Fergie*! C'mon!"

"Oh yeah," April agreed, nodding as if she recognized the song. Jessica grabbed her wrist and pulled April out onto the middle of the dance floor, right under the giant disco ball. As she whirled around and started dancing, she saw Dave standing where she had been, looking hurt and confused.

But she felt more alive than she *ever* had before when she looked around the circle at all the faces laughing and smiling at her. Her whole life, April had wanted to be in the popular crowd—to be one of those girls with no worries other than being pretty and choosing which guy to have a crush on next. And for the first time, it seemed like it was happening to her. Everything she'd wanted when she left for Wellness Canyon eight weeks ago was finally coming true.

April smiled as Jessica grabbed her hands and twirled her around in a circle, Jessica's bangles clinking against each other like chimes in April's ear. April returned the twirl, then stepped out of the way as Jessica whirled around, her blond hair flying. Everyone laughed, the silver reflections from the disco ball flickering across April as she danced. April couldn't help her huge dorky grin. For the first time all summer—no, make that her whole *life*—everything was perfect.

# CHAPTER 37

**DATE:** August 9th

**FOOD:** 1 banana from the dining hall. And a small handful of almonds

**EXERCISE:** Leg raises while reading. Weird new habit.

"HI, HONEY!" WIL'S MOM SCREECHED INTO WIL'S CELL PHONE. Wil put aside *The Perks of Being a Wallflower*, which she had just finished, and lay back on her bed to talk. "We've missed you so much. Are you happy to be coming home?"

"Huh? Oh yeah, totally," Wil answered. For once, she was unsure of how to respond. She'd spent so much time hating Wellness Canyon this summer, but things were different now. Somehow, the whole experience wasn't as terrible as she thought it was going to be.

"So, we'll pick you up tomorrow morning, right? Your father had a wonderful idea to stop off at the beach on the way home to take some photos. Doesn't that sound great? All of our pictures will be so out of date!" Wil's mom sounded so excited that Wil was mildly afraid she would spontaneously combust.

"Oh, Mom, you really don't have to do that. A car service is fine. No need for you guys to come all the way up here and then just turn around and go home," Wil said, pulling her thick Berkeley sweatshirt on over her black American Apparel T-shirt. The T-shirt was the one thing from her parents' care package that she hadn't either given to April or thrown in the lost-and-found box in the Lodge.

"Oh, please. We can't wait to see you. Honey," she said, lowering her voice before going on. "Just how much weight have you lost? What, honey? Hold on, Wil." Wil could tell her mother had put her hand over the receiver. "Okay, okay. I'll ask her. Hi, honey," Wil's mother said to Wil. "Your father wants me to ask what your new BMI is."

Wil rolled her eyes. It was true, she had lost weight, but her parents were so obsessed and . . . constrictive.

"Mom?" Wil said, getting up off the bed and putting on her black Converse. "I . . . uh . . . have to run. We're having some sort of . . . bonfire . . . thing. Last night, you know." She had to do something—anything to get off the phone.

"Okay, honey, good night. See you tomorrow, skinny!" Wil's mom exclaimed, air-kissing into the phone. Wil hung up and sighed. She checked the clock and left her room.

Dew had formed on the grass and Wil dragged her feet as she started the quarter-mile climb on the dirt trail to Huge Rock. Her muscles ached from the Olympics, but she smiled as her newly trim body easily managed the trail. She'd been noticing it more and more each day, and now it felt like she'd been wearing a suit of armor all her life.

Once she was at the top, Wil shone her silver pocket flashlight into the darkness, wanting to give ample warning to any campers making out. Wil sprawled out on the rock where Colin had kissed her so long ago. She felt a little guilty about Colin getting in so much trouble, but she didn't really want to admit it. It wasn't like he got sent home or anything. The thing she *really* felt bad about was that they hadn't thought of the laxative prank earlier.

She pulled a bag of Hershey's Kisses out of her pocket and set it next to her. She had surreptitiously gone back to the 7-Eleven alone to get the bag for April. She couldn't believe she was doing something so cheesy and over-the-top friend-shippy. But she couldn't help herself. She'd never had a friend like April. Even if they hadn't totally liked each other the whole time, being roommates and co-conspirators had kind of led to, well, being *partners*. Wil had been used to feeling like she was alone—against her parents, against the people in her school, against the world. She had never really had a lot of friends. Most kids in her school didn't really understand what it meant to be fat—to feel like that had somehow become part of your identity.

But she and April had been through this whole nasty, grueling summer together, had survived sugar cravings, jock assholes, anal counselors, and awful hikes—and they'd made it out on the other end. Camp friends were one thing, but Wil felt like they'd transcended that. She was really going to miss April when she was gone.

Wil opened the bag and dumped the Kisses out onto the rock, maneuvering them around until they spelled out COLIN SUCKS in the moonlight. Suddenly, she heard some rustling in the leaves. Wil turned toward the noise, expecting to see April, but instead she saw Dave. His gold medal hung around his neck, bouncing against his shirt and tie, and he had an upset look on his face. "Dave? What are you doing? Where's April?"

Dave looked surprised to see her there and sat down, sighing. "Back at the dance. With Jessica, Marci, and Gregg. I think they're drunk." He adjusted his medal and dusted off a spot of dirt from his pant leg. "She's been dancing with those guys and totally ignoring me for the last two hours, but she asked me to tell you that she'll catch up with you later."

Wil kicked some of the Hershey's Kisses and the little foil pieces flew off the rock, glistening in the moonlight for a brief moment before they disappeared from view. She couldn't believe that after everything she and April had been through with Colin, and winning the Olympics, and just, well, relying on each other that April would go right back to where she had started this summer. When all was said and done, April had only changed on the outside—and inside, she was just as rotten and popularity-obsessed as she had always been. Wil got up and put her hands in her pockets, seething now. "Hey, where are you going? Can I have these?" Dave asked, scooping up some of the small foil pyramids.

"Whatever," Wil said. "They were for April, but she's too busy kissing Jessica's butt to actually care." Wil climbed down Huge Rock and stormed back down the trail toward the dance.

# CHAPTER 38

**DATE:** August 9th
**FOOD:** Just some punch
**EXERCISE:** Danced for hours!

APRIL LOOKED AROUND AND NOTICED THAT ONLY THE COOL people were left at the dance—and she was one of them! She shimmied under the blue and purple lights, everyone bobbing their head to the words of the song as it faded. She knew the dance would end soon, but she kept hoping that time wouldn't come. She wished that it was the first day of camp and that she could do it all over again, this time starting out with Jessica and Marci instead of just ending with them.

"Play it again!" Jessica screamed at the DJ, her voice hoarse from singing at the top of her lungs. The punch bowl had long since been drained, cleaned, and put back into the kitchen in the Lodge.

"I'm so glad my roommate didn't come so I could hang out with you!" April shouted to Jessica and Marci over the music. They smiled and then got weird looks on their faces and looked at something behind April.

Suddenly April felt a hard tap on her shoulder and she froze. Finally, she turned around and saw Wil dressed in shorts and a sweatshirt, her tan face flushed with anger. Her nostrils flared a little, and her blue eyes flashed. If April hadn't been afraid that she was about to kill her, she might have thought that Wil actually looked pretty.

"Why didn't you meet me?" Wil asked angrily, her black Converse sneakers planted squarely in the middle of the dance floor.

April smiled nervously at Jessica and Marci, who had stopped dancing and whose faces looked confused. "What?" April asked innocently.

"Why didn't you meet me?" Wil repeated.

April noticed Dave hovering in the background, his medal swinging around his neck, and her panic doubled.

"So I didn't come up and meet you. Who cares?" April said. She was surprised at how much anger she still had bottled up toward beginning-of-the-summer Wil. But April realized that hanging out with Jessica and Marci had brought it all boiling to the surface again.

"Who cares? I care. Which is more than I can say for you. You obviously only care about yourself," Wil screeched, her curly hair bouncing as she talked.

"Wil, I was here, having fun. And you are like . . . not fun." April rolled her eyes toward Jessica and Marci and waited for them to laugh at her joke, but they just stood there in silence.

"Yeah, it sure looks like it's fun enough to be worth blowing off the one person you've spent the whole damn summer with." Wil snorted.

"See, this is what I'm talking about," April said loudly, feeling very warm all of a sudden. The room suddenly began to spin a little and she was surprised at how angry she was becoming.

"These your new friends?" Wil asked, her eyebrows raised. She stuck her hands into the front pocket of her hoodie as she nodded at Jessica and Marci.

"What do you want, Wil?" April felt the situation spiraling out of control as the crowd tightened around them. April's eyes drooped a little and she could feel herself becoming more and more drunk. She just wanted to go back to dancing. Concentrating too much was making her nauseous. She closed her eyes, trying to make the room stop spinning.

"I'm just surprised that they want to be friends with you," Wil said offhandedly, looking up into the corner of the room as she set her mouth into a line. "I mean, it was because of you that they lost today."

A cold chill went up April's spine. Wil smirked at April. "Oh, you mean you didn't tell them about what you did to Colin?"

April felt Jessica and Marci's stare and soon everyone else was staring too, and she went cold. Suddenly, all the lights came on, making the decorations and party dresses look cheap and fake. April blinked and then stared into Wil's icy blue eyes. "It was your idea! All I wanted was to have a good time at camp! *You're* the one who was so intent on making everyone else just as miserable as you are!"

"What's she talking about?" Jessica asked April, gripping her arm for support.

"She's crazy," April tried to explain, searching Jessica's face for some friendly understanding.

"I'm not the one who slipped the laxatives into Colin's protein shake," Wil said, casually running her hands through her hair. "*That's* crazy."

"But it was all your idea," April nearly yelled, her voice cracking. Suddenly, she was conscious of her voice carrying across the whole room. A group of campers had all circled them, watching the fight. "It was all *you*." She pushed her finger into Wil's chest and Wil swiped it away.

"Oh, right, I forgot." Wil answered her calmly, looking like she accused people of sabotage in front of a large audience every day. "*You* just wanted to poison his food. I guess Colin was lucky to get out of camp alive."

Jessica wrinkled her pert little nose and gave April a chilly stare. She just stood looking at her, her bare feet on the dirty wooden floor now covered in streamers and rapidly deflating balloons. "That's *so* not cool, April."

"It's not true," April pleaded with Jessica. She felt her knees start to shake.

Jessica and Marci turned and walked away, leaving April and Wil in the middle of the pack of campers, who were shifting on their feet, waiting for someone to throw the first punch. April looked around, hoping to draw Jessica and Marci back by pleading her innocence, but was horrified to see the girls talking to Melanie, who had just walked in the door to help with the cleanup.

It was all over. April closed her eyes as the crowd parted to let Melanie pass.

"Is this true?" Melanie demanded. She put her hands on her hips and April thought about how out of place Melanie looked in her Wellness Canyon polo shirt, the collar flipped up, as if this wasn't a magical night of dancing and laughing but just another Olympic exercise.

April glanced at Wil, who shot her a look of pure hatred. "Yes," Wil answered.

"I'm stripping you of your medals," Melanie announced, loud enough for everyone to hear. "Cheaters never win, *especially* here at Wellness Canyon."

Dave tried to back away, instinctively covering his medal with his hand.

"Give it to me," Melanie said sternly, holding her hand out to Dave.

Dave looked hurt as he lifted the medal over his head and held it for a moment in the palm of his hand. When he looked up again, April could see that he was on the verge of tears. "That's the first medal I ever won," he said, staring straight into Melanie's eyes. "I won it, fair and square. I don't know what they're talking about. I earned this."

Dave's begging was no use. Melanie grabbed the medal and stuffed it into her pocket like it was a dirty Kleenex.

"Get back to your room," she said to April and Wil. "I'll deal with you later."

April ran out of the building, hearing Wil right on her heels. Her perfect night had dissolved into a complete nightmare. Instead of people staring at her on the dance floor, thinking that she was pretty and popular, they were thinking about what a horrible cheater she was. This was *not* the way the most important summer of her life was supposed to end, and it was all Wil's fault.

"You totally ruined my summer. Happy now?" April snapped over her shoulder, unable to turn and look at Wil. She strained every muscle in her face and throat to keep herself from sobbing.

"Don't worry," Wil answered, her voice dripping with sarcasm. "Jessica wasn't really going to be your friend anyway. She had the whole freaking summer, and you think that just because she's nice to you on the very last day that means she's not going to go back to her own life and forget you ever existed?" Wil whistled softly as they walked through the door of their little room in Franklin. "Please."

April stifled the urge to turn and swing at Wil. She'd never punched anyone in her life and she wasn't going to let Wil drag her down, but she was still fantasizing about it as she climbed into bed. She turned her back to Wil, the room eerily quiet. April planned to wake up early, grab her stuff, and just go. She'd just disappear and never see Wil, Jessica, Marci, or Melanie *ever* again.

# CHAPTER 39

**DATE:** August 10th. Way early.
**FOOD:** Chocolate bar from my dresser.
Think I deserve a treat after
what April did.
**EXERCISE:** Walking to Huge Rock and back.
Alone.

"WAKE UP," A VOICE IN THE DARKNESS SAID. WIL COULDN'T SEE, but she knew it was Melanie.

"Lift your head," another voice—Kevin's?—said from across the room.

As Wil sat up in bed to flip on a light, someone else flicked on the overhead, filling the room with blinding light. "What the hell's going on?" Wil cried as she shielded her eyes with her hand. Melanie grabbed her arm and hauled out her of bed, Wil's bare feet touching the cold floor.

"What the hell are you doing? Stop," April cried as Kevin dragged her out of bed. "This is harassment," she shouted, her hair sticking up in every possible direction.

"You two have one minute to get dressed," Melanie said

as she and Kevin stood out in the hallway. "Then we're coming back in."

April stared at Wil, who stared back at her for a moment before turning away. They were both too furious to say anything and reluctantly started to pull on socks, jeans, and sneakers. Wil wanted to ask her what the hell was happening, but she didn't want to be the first one to speak. Besides, she'd vowed that she would never say another word to April ever again and she wasn't about to break that. She stepped into her sneakers and pulled on her orange Gap hoodie just as Melanie and Kevin reentered the room.

"Put your hands behind your back," Melanie's voice instructed, and Wil obliged. Wil felt a pair of cold handcuffs on her wrists and her heart started beating faster. She assumed this was their punishment but wondered what exactly the punishment entailed. Maybe Melanie was going to haul them out in front of all the other campers to try to humiliate April and Wil like they'd humiliated Colin.

Then Wil felt a cool, silky eye mask slip over her eyes. "Melanie?" her wavery voice asked. "What *is* this?" Melanie didn't say anything, instead pushing Wil in the direction of the doorway.

"You too," Kevin told April. His normally comic voice sounded threatening in the dark, but then again, probably anything seemed threatening when you were blindfolded.

"My parents are gonna sue!" Wil shouted as Melanie and Kevin led them out of Franklin.

Wil could hear a car door opening, and the plastic seat was cool on her legs as she was forced in, April next to her, like a pair of criminals being put in the back of a police car. "Don't worry," Melanie said, starting the engine. "They all signed releases."

Wil closed her eyes behind the eye mask and felt the warm return of sleep as she bounced along the road. She began drifting off and then the car suddenly stopped. The doors swung open and April and Wil were led from the backseat. The eye mask was pulled back and Wil squinted in the fading moonlight at Melanie and Kevin's stony faces. "Where are we?" Wil asked, angrily.

"What you did to Colin was very wrong." Melanie scolded, her hands on her hips.

"Give me a break." Wil snorted, rubbing her eyes. "It was just a prank. On a jerk who totally deserved it." Wil suddenly felt enraged at having her last miserable night at Wellness Canyon interrupted by whatever this lame stunt was.

"You both failed this summer," Melanie said sternly. Kevin crossed his arms, no ounce of leniency in his normally kind face.

"But camp's over," April cried in the darkness. "We both lost weight!" April's voice turned whiny. "We did *our* job. And we're supposed to go home!"

Melanie's eyes met April's. "If you think this was just about losing weight, then you guys need this even more than I thought." She paused, giving Wil an equally cold look. "I want you to think about that as you find your way back."

Melanie looked them both over and shook her head. She climbed back into the Wellness Canyon Jeep as Kevin got behind the wheel. In a flash of dust and moonlight the Jeep was gone, back down what looked like a wide trail. Wil watched the Jeep as it off-roaded down a hill and out of sight. Her eyes adjusted to the dark and she looked around, wondering what on earth they were supposed to do now.

Wil picked a stone up off the ground and hurled it after the Jeep, which was now long gone.

"I can't believe they just left us here," April whined, planting her feet and putting her hands on her hips.

Wil kicked the dusty trail and ignored April. The desert was suddenly extremely dark and she scanned for familiar landmarks. She shuddered when she remembered Melanie's instructions about what to do if lost in the woods. STOP. *Stop, think, observe, and plan.* How about KMA? *Kiss my ass.*

In the distance, a soft glow peeked up over the horizon, illuminating the reddish brown tint of Huge Rock, due north of Wellness Canyon. Wil marched purposefully toward camp, ready to pack her stuff and put the worst summer of her life behind her. For once, she hoped her parents would come early.

"Wait, where are you going?" April clomped along the trail, trying to keep up. "Why are you walking so fast? Wait up."

Wil spun around, freezing April in her tracks. "Where am I going? I'll tell you where I'm going. I'm getting the hell out of here. Away from you." She marched ahead, not waiting for April to respond. Up on the horizon, she could just begin to make out trees and the relief of the surrounding cliffs as the sun crept up. "If you weren't so freaking obsessed with Jessica, Marci, and all them, you'd know that this was the way to camp."

April's jaw dropped open. "I'm not obsessed—"

"Yeah, whatever." Wil flipped her hand in the air. She was so pissed at April she could hardly breathe. "I heard someone call you Jessica's poodle in the dining hall. I didn't tell you because I didn't think it was fair. But it's *way more* than fair."

April's forehead wrinkled in anger. "Who said that?"

"Does it matter?" Wil turned and continued down the trail, the desert landscape casting long shadows in the purplish early morning sunrise.

"You made it up," April accused, lengthening her stride to keep pace with Wil.

Wil stopped again and April took a step back, as if Wil might swing at her. "No, I *didn't* make it up. Just like I didn't make up the fact that Dave likes you." She was already thirsty. Wil wanted to kill Melanie for not leaving them bottles of water. "Didn't you even *notice*? He's been so nice to you all summer, encouraging you during the Olympics—he practically lost his *voice* cheering for you."

"You're crazy." April reached up and knotted her hair into a messy ponytail. "He doesn't *like* me. We're just friends."

"Friends don't show up to walk you to a dance." Wil turned back to the trail. "He was so excited to be at the dance with you, and then you *totally* blew him off. I mean, have you ever *really* looked at Dave? He freaking *adores* you." It pissed Wil off that

April hadn't even noticed Dave. He had been into her from the beginning, but April was too busy drooling over Colin and Jessica to see what was right in front of her eyes. "You can spend your whole life going after guys like Colin, but it's hard to find guys like Dave who really care about you."

April stopped on the trail and stared blankly at Wil.

Wil continued, "I'm going back. Follow me or whatever, don't. I don't care. I can't believe I wasted a summer on you." She charged ahead as the first sliver of red sun peeked up over the cliffs on the horizon.

"Wasted a summer on me? Please! You're lucky that I was even friends with you this summer. You complain so much about your parents, but you're just like them," April shouted. She still stood in the same spot, staring at Wil.

"What?" Wil stopped and turned, her tone turning icy. She was so furious that she began to shake.

"All you do is complain about your parents and all their money and how they just buy you off with presents. But you did the same exact thing to me with that dress. How would you expect me to feel?" April shouted, stomping her foot on the ground as she pressed her hands into her hips.

"Screw you, April! I would never, *ever* want to be friends with a person like you," Wil said coldly. She turned around and power-walked back toward camp.

Wil could hear April's footsteps and what sounded like quiet sobs behind her for the rest of the hike. She mulled the situation over as the sun came up. It soon became bright, and the morning became so warm that the girls had to take off their sweatshirts. Whenever Wil thought of how long she'd planned that end-of-summer moment with the Hershey Kisses up at Huge Rock, she felt as sick as she did the time she'd invited everyone in her third-grade class to her house for a birthday party and only little John Hycner showed up.

The Lodge suddenly came into view and Wil pushed through a clearing, stumbling back into camp behind one of the dorms. She heard April fall, but Wil didn't look back. Wellness Canyon was a buzz of activity—cars were already lined up in the driveway, ready to take the campers back to their normal lives. Wil's parents' limo was not yet one of them. She stopped to look at the mob of campers that had gathered under the Lodge porch hugging, some crying, all saying goodbye, promising to e-mail or call as soon as they got home. She was angry that after all of this, she just felt empty—and just alone as she had when she'd arrived at the beginning of the summer.

April sidled up next to her and they watched the scene. Then they looked at each other and split off in different directions. Wil headed back to Franklin, not caring if she ever saw April again.

# CHAPTER 40

**DATE:** August 10th

**FOOD:** I don't even remember.

**EXERCISE:** Hike from God only knows where.

APRIL DODGED THE CAMPERS STREAMING OUT OF THE LODGE—
she wanted breakfast but couldn't bear the thought of standing in the dining hall line, all the other campers staring at her
because of what she and Wil had done to Colin. They all probably knew about her and Wil being stranded out in the middle
of nowhere, too. She ducked behind Dickinson and took the
long way to Dave's dorm room. April worried that she was too
late, that Dave had already gone, the sad look on his face the last
image April would have of him.

She knocked on Dave's door, holding her breath.

"Come in." She opened the door slowly. Dave had his
duffel bag open on his stripped bed and he was stuffing
T-shirts into it. Paul's side of the room was already bare, and
April realized that she owed him an apology too, though it
was obviously too late now. Dave stopped packing when April
walked in. "Oh. Hey."

247

"Hey." Sudden nerves gripped April and she wondered if she was just going to make the situation worse. "Paul got out early, huh?" She regretted the casual tone in her voice immediately. Dave shrugged and went back to packing. "But I'm glad you're still here. I just wanted to . . . um . . . say that I'm sorry."

"No worries," Dave said curtly as he shoved the last of his clothes into the duffel bag and zipped it. "I kinda figured we'd just end up as friends. That's just how it goes, right?"

April saw a hurt look cross Dave's dark brown eyes and it reminded her of the look he'd had on his face when Melanie took away his medal. "You can't help who you like, can you?" Dave swung his bag over his shoulder and breezed past April and out the door.

April stared at the sad-looking empty room. Then she turned and followed Dave. "Wait." Dave slowed until April caught up and they walked out of the dorm toward the Lodge. "I didn't know. I mean, I didn't see it," she said, glancing up at Dave as they walked, trying to see his face. "I think you're great. Really."

"You don't have to say that." Dave waved to someone on the lawn. "It doesn't matter. We're friends, okay?" He stopped walking and smiled down at her, and April noticed for the first time that he had really beautiful eyes. "I hope we stay in touch, April."

April nodded. "I'd like that." She realized that she really meant it. "And I just want you to know that I *really am* sorry. About the Olympics and all that, but everything else, too."

"Have you talked to Wil?" Dave shifted his duffel from one shoulder to the other. "Because the thing is . . . that's who you should apologize to. She was the one who was really upset last night. More than me."

April thought he was joking and she laughed. "Wil doesn't care about me."

Dave stopped and turned toward her. "You're wrong. When I got up to Huge Rock last night, she was waiting for you. She had all these Hershey's Kisses set out for you. I guess as some kind of thing for surviving the summer." Dave glanced up as a few squealing girls ran past them toward the cars, their backpacks thumping against their backs. "I've never seen someone so sad."

April couldn't believe what Dave was saying. "But she said that they were just lumps of chocolate," April said in a daze, remembering that day at the 7-Eleven.

"What?" Dave asked, not understanding.

"Oh, nothing. I was just . . . thinking." That whole hike back to camp April hadn't been able to figure out why Wil cared so much about how Dave felt about her or even that they'd gotten busted for tainting Colin's protein powder. It didn't make sense. But now April felt like she might throw up.

April looked up and gazed through the window, her eyes following Jessica and Marci as they strode across the lawn toward the driveway. She looked up at Dave, who was still staring at her. She blushed, remembering the look on his face when she'd denied he was her date. Suddenly, she had an idea.

"Come on," April said, dragging Dave along by his sleeve.

"What? I don't kno—," Dave complained.

April pulled Dave out to the porch and waited until Jessica and Marci got closer, and then she took a step toward Dave. She stood on her tiptoes and kissed him. Right on his lips. Right in front of Jessica and Marci and anyone else who happened to turn their head at that moment.

His lips felt soft beneath hers, and as she pulled away, she saw a look of astonishment in his eyes. "*That* was my first kiss," she said breathlessly, staring up into his eyes.

Dave grinned and touched her cheek. "Go find Wil," he said, suddenly serious. "I'll e-mail you when I get home." He reached down and hugged her, and then April ran off. She hoped it wasn't too late.

# CHAPTER 41

**DATE:** August 10th

**FOOD:** Did I eat breakfast? I don't remember.

**EXERCISE:** Long-ass hike with April. I am SO done with this.

WIL SIGHED WITH RELIEF WHEN SHE SPOTTED HER PARENTS' limousine idling in the long Wellness Canyon driveway. Then her heart sank when reality set in: her parents were in their coordinated tracksuits, looking as sleek and fit as ever as they leaned against the side of the car, scanning the crowd of campers for Wil and whispering to each other. But at this point, she just wanted to get the hell away from Wellness Canyon as fast as she could.

Wil approached the limo. She'd taken a quick shower after Melanie's ridiculous attempt to teach them a lesson and had thrown on a pair of jean shorts that she'd snitched from the lost and found because most of her clothes, even the smaller sizes that her parents had optimistically packed in her suitcase for her, no longer fit. Her black Nirvana T-shirt, which was once so

251

tight it made her parents cringe when she wore it in public, now
hung on her like a tent.

Her mom spotted her first, and when she saw Wil walking
toward them, her mouth dropped open.

"Oh, my," her mother yipped, holding her tanned hand
over her mouth. She looked like she might start crying. "You
look so . . ." She stared at Wil wordlessly. The chauffeur, a new
one Wil didn't recognize, took her bag and put it in the trunk.

"Come here," her father said, knocking the brim of his
Dodgers cap against Wil's forehead as he scooped her up. "You
look terrific, honey." He spun her around in a circle. "Wow, I
can get my arms all the way around you."

"I want to try," her mother squealed. Wil caught a whiff
of her mother's perfume as she put her bony arms around Wil.
Wil's mom gave her a small squeeze but also used her arms as
calipers to measure just how much weight Wil had lost. "It's
amazing." Her mother turned to her father, her thin lips beam-
ing. "Let's make a donation to Wellness Canyon this year. In
Wil's name. A scholarship or something."

"Great idea," her father said, placing his hand on Wil's
shoulder. Immediately, she thought of the handcuffs Melanie
had put on them last night—even with those around her wrists,
she hadn't felt as trapped as she did right now. "Are you ready
to go home?"

Wil nodded. The chauffeur held the door and her parents climbed in. Wil gave one last look around, marking all the
things she'd be glad to never see again: the fake modern lodge,

the wide green lawn, even the stately buildings that had housed them all summer long. She'd deny ever having spent the summer at Wellness Canyon if anyone asked, like a rock star lying about rehab.

As Wil ducked down into the limo, ready to put the camp in the rearview mirror, she saw April racing toward her out of the corner of her eye. She was still wearing the jeans and sweatshirt she'd had on last night, her unwashed hair falling loose around her shoulders.

"Wil, wait!" April slowed as she approached the limo, resting her hand on the trunk as she felt her way along the car, catching her breath. "Wait a minute."

Wil got out of the car and stared blankly at April. Wil still felt jilted—she'd spent the entire summer with April, practically three meals a day, activities, spare time. Their beds were eight feet away from each other, for heaven's sake. And April had still chosen to hang out with some insipid girls who didn't even know her last name instead of meeting up with Wil on the final night of the summer. "What do you want?"

April swiped at a thin lock of auburn hair that fell in front of her eyes. Her freckles had really come out in the sun, and her cheeks were flushed pink like she'd just applied way too much blush. "Dave told me about Huge Rock." April shook her head sadly, and her mouth was twisted into a frown. "I didn't know. Why didn't you say something? I would've skipped the entire dance."

"No, you wouldn't have," Wil answered, aware that the

chauffeur and her parents were probably listening. "It doesn't matter anyway. Don't worry about it." Her voice was casual, in the coldest way she could manage. "Just, you know, have a nice life."

Wil crawled into the limo, bouncing along the plush leather seating as the chauffeur slammed the door dramatically in April's face. The limo glided slowly toward the gates. Wil looked over her shoulder and noticed that April was still standing where she'd left her, staring after the car.

"Was that one of your new friends? Why didn't you introduce us?" Wil's father asked, looking out the window at April as he patted Wil's hand.

"Not exactly, Dad," Wil said, pulling her hand away from her father's.

"Forget the old commercial idea." Her father clapped as if the idea had just come to him, although she could tell from the way he brought it up that they'd been discussing it the whole way down here. "Let's put up a before picture of Wil and then an after picture. It can be all about family health." He placed his hand on Wil's bare knee and she stared at it as if it belonged to a stranger. "Like: If families work out together, then everyone wins."

"Ooh, I know the perfect picture." Her mother tapped a pale pink nail against her temple. "Remember that picture of you on our vacation to Cabo? I've never seen a more miserable human being. It's perfect."

Wil's stomach sank to her feet as she listened to her parents prattle on. The limo passed through the Wellness Canyon gates and out onto the main road. Wil looked through the window and spotted the wooded trail leading to the clearing where she and April had ditched the hike to go to the 7-Eleven. She wanted to laugh as she remembered how scared April had been of getting caught.

*We were friends,* Wil realized. She thought of April the second time at the 7-Eleven, laughing as she crushed up the laxatives in her shoes. Then she remembered going shopping and talking about how Colin was their first kiss. And sneaking around in the dark, trying to put the powder in Colin's Nalgene bottle. They really *had* been friends. She had just never really put it together, and now she was going back to Malibu where there was no April. Where there were no friends at all.

Wil felt something wet in her eyes, and before she could do anything about it, a stream of tears ran down her face.

# CHAPTER 42

**DATE:** August 10th
**FOOD:** ½ of a banana I found in my room
**EXERCISE:** Packing. Thank God.

APRIL BOARDED THE IDLING SHUTTLE VAN WITH HER DUFFEL BAG, tears stinging her eyes as she climbed in. The van was full of campers, and the only available seat was up front. She settled in, arranging her bag at her feet while they waited for the driver, who was chatting in the driveway with Melanie.

The summer had been a success—she'd lost the weight she'd wanted to lose—but she still felt so unsatisfied. The delicious scene April had crafted where Olivia St. James and all the others back home would do a double take on seeing her had lost all its power. She didn't care what Olivia thought. She didn't care what anyone thought.

April sighed. That wasn't entirely true. She *did* care what her mother thought, actually—she wanted her to think she was a good person, not the kind of person who just tried to make the popular kids like her.

April sniffled and tried to keep herself from breaking into

full-fledged sobs. She had done what she'd set out to do this summer—she had lost all that weight and now she was going back home as a brand-new person. But just on the outside. On the inside, she felt as rotten as ever. Wil had said some terrible things to her, but she wasn't wrong.

Tears streamed down April's face and she looked straight out the window, feeling exhausted. A dragonfly settled on the windshield, its wings beating in the sunlight, though none of the other campers seemed to notice. April stared at the dragonfly until she looked past it and saw Wil running up the long driveway.

And then, suddenly, she realized Wil was running to *her*. She jumped up and stepped off the bus and Wil, not even out of breath, threw her arms around her, almost knocking them both to the ground.

"I'm sorry too." Wil wiped away a tear and took a step back. "I should have said it before, but . . . I'm kind of, you know, stubborn. I was horrible this whole summer."

April wiped her hand under her eyes. "No, no. I was awful. *I'm* sorry."

Wil hugged April tightly and they just stood there, smiling and laughing.

"C'mon. I'll take you home." Wil grabbed April's hand and they walked back toward the gates. The black limo reversed slowly up the driveway until it reached them. The passenger's side window unrolled.

"Who's this?" a good-looking man wearing a red tracksuit asked pleasantly.

Wil put her arm around April's shoulders, something April could never have imagined her doing before. It felt surprisingly comfortable. "This is my roommate—I mean, my friend, April."

"Hi." April smiled nervously.

"And these," Wil said dramatically, gesturing toward two people visible in the limousine window, "are my parents." Wil gave April a small smile. April was grateful she wasn't wearing the L.A.M.B. yoga suit that had come in Wil's care package.

"Hi, April," Wil's mother said, leaning over her husband and smiling out the window. April noticed for the first time that they were wearing coordinating spandex tracksuits. "It's so nice to meet a friend of Wil's."

"It's so nice to meet you," April responded, smiling first at Wil's parents and then at Wil. "I've heard so much about you."

"Um, Dad? April's from San Luis Obispo and, well, she came on the bus," Wil told her parents while shifting April's duffel bag from one hand to the other. "I know it's the opposite direction, but I don't know. I was thinking that maybe we could . . ."

"Sure." Her father smiled, opened the car door, and climbed out. Up front, the chauffeur scrambled out of the driver's seat and took April's bag from Wil. "After you," Wil's father said, bowing as he held the door open for April.

April chuckled and got in, scooting over to make room for Wil beside her. Wil's parents jumped in and the driver started up the car just as the shuttle bus roared past them to the end of the driveway, signaling before it turned, and then disappeared from view. The limo drove through the gates and Wil smiled as she reached into her pocket and pulled out three shiny Hershey's Kisses.

April felt like she was going to start crying all over again, so she didn't say anything. She took one of the Kisses, unwrapped it, and popped it in her mouth, letting the creamy sweetness creep over her tongue. Wil took one, too, and smiled as she bit into it. She took April's arm in her own as the Wellness Canyon gate grew small in the rearview mirror and they drove back out into the real world.

April smiled as Wil's parents began peppering the girls with questions about the summer. The Southern California sunlight beamed down through the open sunroof, and April thought that it was true: nothing—that Hershey's Kiss included—was as sweet as being a brand-new skinny April. But nothing—nothing at all—was sweeter than leaving Wellness Canyon with a new best friend by her side.

# PRETTY FACE
## MARY HOGAN

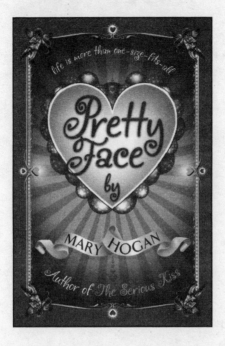

The girl with the pretty face. That's Hayley. A funny girl.
A friend but nobody's girlfriend.

From the author of *The Serious Kiss* comes a hilarious and
heartbreaking new novel for every girl who's ever felt
uncomfortable in her own skin. Hayley is one of those girls,
but this summer everthing is going to change. She's off to Italy,
where she'll discover what real pizza tastes like, what real
beauty looks like, and maybe even what true amore can be.

Price: £5.99
ISBN: 978-1-84738-228-3

# THE ASHLEYS
## MELISSA DE LA CRUZ

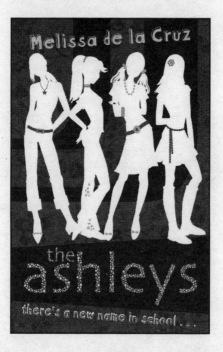

Meet the Ashleys – rulers of Miss Gamble's Preparatory School
for Girls, gorgeous, rich, impeccably dressed, and, of course,
all named Ashley.

Meet Lauren Page – pretty, but slightly geeky, she's been going to
the same school as the Ashleys for as long as she can remember,
and they barely even notice she's alive.

But her parents got the trend wrong when they chose her
name, because Lauren is so obviously an Ashley. And this year,
everything is going to change.

Price: £5.99
ISBN: 978-1-84738-259-7